EXPLORING THE
UNKNOW
Consciousness is the One and Only Reality

January No. 38
1967

Robert A. W. Lowndes

SAUCERIAN PUBLISHER

ISBN:978-1-7366564-4-0

© 2021 Saucerian Publisher

Prologue

It is generally a good idea to return to the classics in any genre. This also goes for UFO literature. Rereading a book after ten or twenty years is a rewarding experience. You will discover new data and ideas you didn´t notice before. The reason, of course, is that you are, in many ways, not the same person reading the book the second or third time. Hopefully you have advanced in knowledge, experience, intellectual and spiritual discernment. A good starting point is to reread the UFO classics in order to understand the deeper mystery involved in what happened during that era.

1947 is considered by most historians of the United States as the year when the Cold War begun with the implementation of the "Truman Doctrine" to contain the propagation of world Communism, which give rise to the anti-communist hysteria of the following years. Also, 1947 was the year when the first UFO sightings were reported in the summer.

EXPLORING THE UNKNOW was published bi-monthly by Robert A. W Lowndes as Editor at New York, New York under the banner of the Health Knowledges Inc. This publication was a forum for Fortean experience and saucer sightings.

Robert Augustine Ward "Doc" Lowndes (September 4, 1916 – July 14, 1998) was an American science fiction author,and editor. He was known best as the editor of Future Science Fiction, Science Fiction, and Science Fiction Quarterly, among many other crime-fiction, western, sports-fiction, and other pulp and digest sized magazines for Columbia Publications. Among the most famous writers he was first to publish at Columbia was mystery writer Edward D. Hoch, who in turn would contribute to Lowndes's fiction magazines as long as he was editing them. Lowndes was a principal member of the Futurians. His first story, "The Outpost at Altark" for Super Science in 1940, was written in collaboration with fellow Futurian Donald A. Wollheim.

In 1963, Lowndes initiated the Magazine of Horror (1963–1971) for Health Knowledge Inc., which mixed reprints with new stories.The magazine was popular and spawned several companion magazines: Startling Mystery Stories, Famous Science Fiction (both 1966) Weird Terror Tales (1969) and Bizarre Fantasy Fiction (1970). Lowndes also edited two non-fantastic-fiction magazines for the company, Thrilling Western Magazine (1967) and World Wide Adventure (1967), along with the speculative nonfiction titles they published. However, the collapse of Health Knowledge in 1971 ended these magazines. Startling Mystery Stories was notable for carrying the first stories of Stephen King, and F. Paul Wilson. Lowndes subsequently went on to work on the Gernsback Publications' non-fiction magazine, Sexology.

Saucerian Publisher was founded with the mission of promoting books in Science Fiction. Our vision is to preserve the legacy of literary history by reprint editions of books which have already been exhausted or are difficult to obtain. Our goal is to help readers, educators and

The topics covered in this publication are: DID THE PHARAOHS BUILD STONEHENGE? ; HINTS ON MEDIUMISTIC DEVELOPMENT ;FLYING SAUCERS AND THE CONTCT ENIGMA ;HEALING SPIRITS ;THE GREAT EXILE

Great, but unpretentious, this edition is a rare symbol by itself of what was going in the dawn of the modern UFO phenomena.

Editor,
Saucerian Publisher, 2021

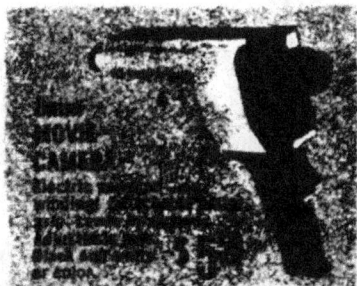

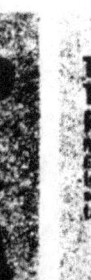

Buy Below Wholesale

Start your own BIG PROFIT Home Import Business...

Import bargains by the thousands give you
profit opportunities beyond your wildest
dreams. Men—women start now in your
own Home Import Business, full or part
time. Cash in now without previous experience or capital investment. You can make
your first import order 10 minutes after
you get my proven drop ship plan. These
bargains and thousands more go quick to
stores, mail order operators, premium
users, friends, others.

DISCOVER SECRETS OF IMPORT
The Profits are All Yours!

Plan reveals everything to start you importing
immediately. Gives you free membership in
International Traders—famous world wide organization that puts you in direct contact with sup-
pliers abroad. It's easy to buy below wholesale
when we show you how. Rush coupon today for
my FREE BOOK. "How to Import and Export"
—get details about thousands of amazing buys.
Airmail reaches me overnight.

EXPLORING THE UNKNOWN

"Consciousness is the One and Only Reality"

Volume 7   Number 2

Robert A. W. Lowndes, *Editor*

Editorial Consultants:

Geraldine Cummins   Jerryl L. Keane, Ph.D.

CONTENTS FOR JANUARY

(Contents for January — continued from page 4)

STRANGE

DEPARTMENTS

SPECIAL SERVICE

EXPLORING THE UNKNOWN, Vol. 7, No. 2, January 1967 (whole number 38). Published bi-monthly by Health Knowledge, Inc. Executive and editorial offices at 119 Fifth Avenue, New York 8, N. Y. Annual subscription (6 issues) $2.50 in the U. S., Canada and Pan American Union. Foreign $3.00. Manuscripts and art material accompanied by stamped, self-addressed envelopes will be carefully considered, but the publisher and editors will not be responsible for loss or damage. © 1965 by Health Knowledge, Inc. All rights reserved under Universal International and Pan American copyright conventions. Printed in U. S. A.

The Ignorant Explorer

". . . nothing but pure wa of bees would do. On one poi authorities were unanimou the wax must be gathered fro the combs of bees who had fe on Mount Caucasus — and n where else." from *The Phœ nix and the Mirror,* k Avram Davidson.

HERE IS science: an effect wanted, the cause sought ar isolated. Experiments are mad First it is found that the effe can be produced only by tl pure wax of bees; then it found that the wax of bees fro one locality is not the san as the wax of bees from anoth locality. And only the wax bees from one particular loca ity seems to have the desire ingredients. The data is collec ed and written in an instructio manual: follow these pro cedures and you will get the results.

And here is superstition can you see it? Can you s science trembling upon tl brink of superstition in the par graph quoted?

When does science met morphosize into superstition Why?

Because men stop askin

vhy"; because they become
ntent with a partial answer.

Why *only* the pure wax of
es? Was an attempt made
break down this pure wax
id see if any of the separate
ments could be eliminated
thout destroying the virtue of
oducing the desired effect?
ie *only* might be correct —
rtainly it might be correct in
day when the necessary soph-
tication of what we now know
as a chemical analysis just
asn't there. It might not have
en possible in the actual time
rresponding to the mythical
edieval period of Davidson's
tarming fantasy about the
gendary Vergil (not the real
uthor of the *Aeneid*, but the
gend of him that grew up in
ie Middle Ages) but the point
that the question wasn't asked
fter a while.

Why from the combs of bees
ho had fed on Mount
aucasus — and nowhere else?
id anyone examine the terri-
>ry to see if there were par-
cular things the bees fed on
tere which were not found in
very other place — but might
e found in some?

No. A certain sort of magic
rtue was assumed to be in the
ire wax; a certain sort of
agic virtue was assumed to
e in Mount Caucasus — so why
aste your time analyzing wax,

(Turn to Page 121)

Did The Pharaohs Build Stonehenge?

by DON MacCLURE

Certainly the engineering skills which brought forth the pyramids could have been used to construct that awesome monument in Wiltshire, England. And we are beginning to realize that the ancients traveled much farther than anyone might have suspected a century or so ago.

"EGYPT CLAIMS STONEHENGE! ARCHAELOGIST SAYS PHARAOHS BUILT OUR MOST CHERISHED NATIONAL MONUMENT."

Those headlines shocked every Briton to his traditionally calm foundations some years ago. The Suez debacle still rankled at the time, and a British Member of Parliament described Egypt's tongue-i cheek claim to Stonehenge as "damnable piece of effrontery Britons agreed with him a poured verbal scorn upon t head of Egypt's Preside Nasser.

Yet there happens to be ju: fication for Egypt's contenti that Stonehenge should lega and historically belong to h One of Britain's foremost :

The Sphinx and one of the Pyramids at Gizeh, Egypt
(before lower part of Sphinx was excavated).

chaeologists and Orientalists, Dr. Rendel Harris, confirmed it by announcing that he had discovered the site of an Egyptian settlement in Wiltshire, the county in which Stonehenge stands. His theories, based on this discovery, turned out to be the most startling ever put forward to account for the origin of that grim and naked monument to early man which stands in the heart of Salisbury Plain, England, defying weather, time, and mankind's puny efforts to probe its secrets.

Among the other suggestions that have been put forward down the centuries are that Stonehenge is not the work of human hands at all, but the fruit of the magic of Merlin, and that the gigantic stones were brought from Africa by giants; that it is the tomb of the heroic Queen Boadicea; that it was a Roman temple, and that it witnessed the gory rights of Druids offering human sacrifices.

Yet even these pale in fascination before the thought that this great monument might be the work of the servants of the Egyptian Pharaohs; and perhaps, after all, when the evidence is considered, it is not so fantastic as the English would like to believe.

Dr. Harris has suggested that the builder of Stonehenge was King Arthur's Merlin, whose real name was Meri-An ("Beloved of Osiris"). He identified Arthur with the god Osiris, and Queen Guinevere with the goddess Isis, and decided that the "Robin Hood" whose name is given to two barrows or earthworks close to Stonehenge was really Ra-Bennu, the sun-god and sun-bird of Egypt.

Other leading archaeologists admit that it is very strange that Dr. Harris's studies should lead him to associate Merlin with Stonehenge, for, as mentioned earlier, legend asserts that he helped in the building of the monument.

The story goes that Ambrosius Aurelianus (who lived about the same time as King Arthur is reputed to have flourished), leader of the Britons against the Saxon chief Hengist, wanted to set up a memorial to those of his men slain in battle.

By advice and with the aid of Merlin, who possessed magical powers, he removed the stones of the Giants' Dance from Kildare, Ireland (where, according to an ancient chronicler, they had been deposited by giants who had taken them from Africa,) and set them up on the site of Stonehenge.

DR. HARRIS suggested that Egyptian settlers came up the River Avon from Bristol and established themselves where the Manors of Great and Little Chalfield are today, near Bradford-on-Avon, Wiltshire. The former has a church didicated to St. Catherine, believed to be Catherine of Alexandria, Egypt.

The syllable "chal" is the equivalent of the Egyptian "tcher" or "tchar" one of the several dual names of the goddesses Isis and Nephthys. These goddesses crop up again at Heytesbury, . England, for "Heyte" is the Egyptian "Heyti", another of their dual names. Then, Harrow-on-the-Hill is another link with Horus, for Harrow conserves "Heru", the Egyptian name for Horus, the child of Isis. Harrogate, too, is believed to be Heru Khart, or "Horus the Child".

But Egyptian archaeologists claim, if all these seem too conjectural, we have only to cross the famous Salisbury Plain to find evidence a little more tangible. First of all, there are numerous ancient burial places on Salisbury Plain, and many of these have been carefully excavated. There has been found in quite a number of them a distinctive piece of blue cloth identified by most eminent Egyptologists with an Egyptian fabric of 1500 to 1200 B.C.

Furthermore there have been unearthed at least two examples of gold-rimmed amber bosses, practically identical with a brooch from Knossos in Crete, dated by Sir Arthur Evans, the celebrated archaeologist who has done much work in that island dealing with lost civilizations, around 1500 B.C.

Now students of Stonehenge believe that it was not built earlier than 1800 B.C., and at that time there must have been trade routes for the bearers of the trinkets. Implements of bronze, too, were brought. So Professor George Engleheart has said "the inference is not wholly visionary", and that if this route to the eastern end of the Mediterranean did exist, "There is no demonstrable impossibility of the importation from abroad of an advisory master mason for Stonehenge."

Where was he likely to have come from? There is only one answer — Egypt, site of the most gigantic of the ancient world's structures, the Pyramids.

To a mason who had inherited the knowledge of how the Pyramids had been built, the erection of a monument like Stonehenge, even though the largest stones weigh 26 tons on the average, would not present too great a difficulty.

It is feasible, too, that such a man would have brought assistants with him, and possibly these men may have settled in Britain, for the building of Stonehenge was not a matter of months.

Probably it took several years to complete, for, when in its entirety, it was a most impressive monument, with two huge circles of stones and inside them two horse-shoe shaped arrangements of other stones. There were great earthworks, too.

Thus, after all, there may be much truth in the Egyptian claim and the theory of Dr. Harris that the Egyptians had at least a hand in the building of Stonehenge.

ONE OF THE latest theories about Stonehenge is that

the inner part was roofed over by wooden beams plastered together with earth. Supporting this, it is obvious that the site of Stonehenge, wide open to the winds, would seem very unsuitable for the establishment of an unsheltered sacred place, a roofless temple. But if covered, the whole thing appears reasonable and in conformity with the common idea of a temple, with its series of enclosures and its general resemblance to an inhabited building.

A people able to handle great stones up to 40 tons in weight would have found little difficulty in handling the thirty-foot beams required.

Innumerable mysteries still surround this ancient monument of a vanished people. Why did they take the trouble to drag some of the stones from Wales? What gods did they worship within their stony barrier? Why was the monument set up in the midst of the great plain, far wilder than it is today?

There are written records which show that Stonehenge was known to the Greeks of the fourth century, B.C. This, the earliest existing reference to any Monument in Britain, is contained in the writings of Diodorus Siculus, a much-respected and painstaking Greek historian. Says Siculus: "Opposite to the land of the Celts there exists in the ocean an island, not smaller than Sicily, inhabited by Hyperboreans. They honor Apollo more than any other deity. A sacred enclosure is dedicated to him in the island, as well as a magnificent circular temple adorned with many rich offerings."

Considering the great antiquity of Stonehenge, legends about it are strangely few. One story, however, concerns the Hale Stone, or Friar's Heel, over which the sun rises on Midsummer Day. The Devil, it is said, noticed a collection of huge stones while traveling in Ireland. He was moved by the spirit of mischief to pick them up and carry them to Salisbury Plain, telling himself gleefully that their mysterious appearance there would puzzle men for centuries to come.

But he was caught in the act of settling them down by a wandering friar, who fled on recognizing him. The devil hurled a stone at the holy man, and struck him on the heel. A curious indentation on the stone is supposed to have been caused by the impact.

More than one archaeologist has suggested that some of the stones actually did come from Ireland, for although Stonehenge consists mainly of sarsen stones indigenous to Wiltshire, it also contains a number of so-called "foreign" stones which are unlike any found within a hundred miles of Salisbury Plain.

Similar stones exist in Cornwall, Devonshire, Cumberland, Shropshire, and Brittany, with the result that all these parts have been suggested as their possible source, but it is now generally agreed that they were quarried by whoever built Stonehenge, in Pembrokeshire, where there are stones that match them perfectly.

How did the ancients manage to transport them over a distance of 180 miles from the other side of the Bristol Channel? Nobody has ever been able to solve that problem for certain, or, in fact, be sure why they were brought to Stonehenge from so far afield. Perhaps they were the sacred stones of a conquered wandering tribe. Perhaps they were spoils of war brought home in triumph by the conquerors. It is unlikely that we shall ever know for certain.

THE EXPERTS can tell that these stones were not cut to shape until they reached Stonehenge, for many chippings from them have been found in the earth around. The most widely accepted theory is that they were dragged to their present site on sledges by teams of slaves.

But that method of transportation would not have been possible in the case of the large sarsen stones. These huge boulders were probably moved from the surrounding countryside on rollers formed out of tree trunks.

The stone may have been cut by means of simultaneous blows with mauls applied by several men standing in line. Stone hammers and quartzite pebbles were used for dressing them, and these primitive tools achieved a more perfect finish than even the modern mason's chisel can produce.

The builders of Stonehenge were not content simply to balance the lintel stones on their uprights. These stones were joined by tenons and mortices worked into them, while the ends of certain lintels were attached to others by means of a dovetailing arrangement known as the "toggle" joint. If these measures had not been adopted it is very doubtful whether any of the lintels would have remained in place to our day.

The tools employed in the cutting and dressing of the stones were dropped into convenient holes as they became unfit for use. Many have been found in the course of excavation at Stonehenge.

These include axes of flint and sarsen, hammer axes edged on one side and flat on the other, rounded and flat hammer stones weighing between one pound and nearly seven pounds, and sarsen mauls varying in weight from forty pounds to sixty-four pounds, as well as numerous fragments of picks made from deer horn.

It is probable that after the holes for the stones had been scooped out they were tipped into them direct from their rollers and then pulled into an upright position by ropes, an operation that must have required the efforts of some two hundred men.

For the hoisting of the lintels, it is likely that sloping mounds of earth were built up round the uprights until these were completely hidden, and that the horizontal stones were then slid or rolled up the mounds.

The majority of the larger stones at Stonehenge have fallen. The trio forming the largest group of all crashed in 1620, and those which were next in size came to earth during a sudden thaw in 1727, partly as the result of some gypsies digging a shelter for themselves at the foot of one of the uprights. The concussion of that fall is said to have been felt a mile away.

Other ancient stone monuments exist in many parts of the world but none combine such an assortment of mysterious and interesting features as Stonehenge. The famous stones of Carnac, in Brittany, are not comparable because they stand in alignment. The stone circles at Avebury, and Ballynoe, North Ireland, are arranged in a different manner; and neither these nor any other circular formations can boast the "enclosed" structures — horizontal stones resting on supports that we see at Stonehenge. The most remarkable dolmen, as this form of primitive structure is called, comparable with Stonehenge stands near Antequera in Spain, and consists of twenty-six supports and five overhead stones.

Ruined dolmens are found all over Europe, and also exist

in Egypt, Asia, Australia and South America.

Some archaeologists believe that all these monuments were erected by members of the same tribe, who roamed the world before the continents were divided by seas, but the geologists deny this. They say, for example, that although Britain was joined to the rest of Europe some considerable time after the seas had divided other parts of the world, even this joint was sundered many thousands of years before the Stone Age.

The only part of the riddle of Stonehenge and its ruined replicas all over the world that does not remain a mystery is that man, from the beginning of time, has felt an urge to provide future generations with evidence of his existence — a purpose best served by a material as enduring as stone.

THE RECKONING

When we score your ballots, we not only note the order in which **you** listed the contents of the issue, but relate it to the ballots previously received, so that we can tell at a glance, any moment, exactly how the issue stands now in relation to the way it stood before. Almost every ballot results in some shifts, and it is particularly interesting to watch the contention for first place. Sometimes it's a runaway for one item from the first; other times it's nip and tuck all the way with a few contendors changing place frequently. And sometimes one item will hold the lead for a long time, finally being nosed out at the end. That is what happened this time. Our winner gradually reduced the lead of the (finally) second place item, coming in ahead with the final ballot. Here is the pay-off listing.

(1) **Psychism vs. Mediumship,** by Jerryl L. Keane, Ph.D.; (2) **"Folklore" of the Famous,** by Harold Steinour; (3) **What Are Miracles?** (editorial); (4) **Queen of Morn** by Marie Harlowe tied with **TV Test for Automatism;** (5) a 3-way tie: **The Ignorant Explorer, Books,** and **The Eyrie;** (6) **Fort's Forte,** by Gaston Burridge; (7) **Your Future—It's in the Cards!;** (8) **Healing Today;** (9) **How Write You Are!**

Hints On Mediumistic Development

by URSULA ROBERTS
(author of *The Spiritual Healing Teach-In*)

This essay originally appeared as a pamphlet, printed by Beagley Brothers, Ltd., Dorchester Road, Northolt Park, Middlesex, England, and is reprinted here by arrangement with the author. Dr. Keane said of it in her review: "It is incredibly refreshing, after wading through pages and reams of intellectualized mish-mash and jargon regarding the existence, nature and meaning of the psychic faculties by well-meaning but confused people, to turn to a **real** authority on the subject . . . one whose authority is based on over 30 years of developing, teaching others, demonstrating, healing and exercizing, for the benefit of others, not for her own aggrandisement." Because upon reading the pamphlet we not only found that Dr. Keane was not exaggerating, but it was the first brief essay on the subject which was not only clear but made excellent sense to this editor, we felt that it was well worth making the effort to see if we could share it with you. Whether you agree is up to you, but we feel that, agree or disagree, you will know what it is you agree or disagree with — which cannot be said about all writing on this subject.

CHAPTER I

PRACTICAL PREPARATION

MEDIUMS ARE those whose psychic senses are so acute that they can register the presence of beings belonging to the non-physical world; and interpret the wishes and information which such beings desire to impart to people still in the body in this physical world. The medium's contact with the other world denizens may result in mediumship of varying forms, ranging from levitation of physical objects to mental mediumship such as inspirational speaking, clairvoyance or clairaudience; from the healing of dire illness to prophetic utterances such as the fore-telling of the future; from the trance-control by a highly evolved spirit speaking in a foreign language through the medium's lips to a degree in which the medium just knows that something is about to occur.

The form which the mediumship may take is not very important; what matters is the way in which the medium responds to the impulsion of the spirits. A good description of a medium is in the words: The spirit caused the medium to speak — or see, or write, or whatever other act may be the medium's reactions to the compulsion of the spirit entity.

A really sensitive medium may be used in a variety of ways at different times, though it is usual for one faculty to be developed to a higher degree of responsiveness, and occasionally this one faculty may become so strong that the other powers fall into abeyance. It is my opinion that good mediumship can manifest all the varied forms of phenomena. During the period of development a mediumship often passes from one phase to another. One can watch a potential medium sometimes sensing spirit contacts by hearing, sometimes by the seeing of symbols, sometimes by entrancement of the medium by the spirit entity.

It is wrong for the *developing* medium to want to mould the mental mediumship so that it is forced into one specific channel, at this stage the sensitive should be content to "be a medium" and not wish to be known as a clairvoyant, clairaudient or trance medium. It is sufficient that the spirits can make their influence felt and the sole desire on the part of the medium should be "May I become more responsive!" Unfortunately this seldom happens, for the great majority of developing mediums have in their minds a model of the medium whom they admire, and unconsciously they tend to mould their mediumship so that it conforms to the kind which their model uses. The motto of the young medium could well be "Use me, but use me in *your* way, not mine."

I THINK one of the wisest things I ever heard was said by a medium in my own circle, when she answered one of the other sitters by saying: "Oh, I don't just want to be as good a medium as Ursula, I want to be a better one!" She was a wise woman, for she was not allowing her mind to be moulded into one specific channel and since she spoke those words she has developed into an outstandingly good spiritual healer and clairvoyant. Another person who was sitting in the circle at the same time said: "If I can be half as good as Ursula, I shall be content." I am sorry to say that her responsiveness to spirit contact has not become really perfect although years have passed since she made that remark. I think it is because she tried to make her mediumship

conform to a pattern instead of trying to learn how to respond more sensitively to the spirit influences. In my own case, as a young medium, I went to a meeting at which Mrs. Estelle Roberts was demonstrating her clairvoyant faculty. Immediately I felt that this was the kind of way in which *my* mediumship ought to develop. I tried to "get" names and addresses of the places where spirit people used to live and completely thwarted the development of healing which the spirit guides were trying to bring about at that time.

It is most important that all mediums should realize the part their own consciousness plays in the use and development of mediumship, for is it not true that all spirit impulsions are interpreted by the medium's consciousness? Good mediumship comes, not with the elimination of the medium's consciousness but with the development of the consciousness into a state where it can most readily respond to the wishes of the spirit operators. Many developing mediums have the idea that they should not be aware of what the spirits are trying to bring through. It is a good thing to remember, at the very start of your development, that you will develop a more acute state of awareness, and your cooperation with the spirits will come about as you learn to re-act more readily to their wishes through this heightened awareness.

HOW DOES ONE prepare for this state of spirit awareness? I think the steps are simply explained as coming to pass in three stages. Firstly by joining a good circle composed of a number of earnest people. Secondly by learning how to expand the aura so that it blends with the aura of the whole circle. Thirdly, learning how to control and direct the thoughts and emotions in a constructive manner.

Many people ask whether they can develop mediumship without joining a circle. It is possible for them to do so, but it is not wise, for the blended aura of a group of people serves to create a protective power around a developing medium. There are no age limits fixed for the desirability of sitters in a circle. Ages can range from seventeen years to seventy-nine, so long as the health of the sitters is fairly good. People often ask whether there are diseases which debar a person from making a good

sitter. I think the answer should be, any disease which causes a debilitated state in the body, with total lack of energy and corresponding moods of depression. Neurasthenics should not be allowed in a circle where a medium is developing, because their moods tend towards mental restlessness, their emotions blossom from self-pity and their auras tend to close in towards themselves, rather than opening out with the flow of auric vitality which is required to help the circle as a whole. Bodily ailments which do not affect the vitality of the person need not affect the circle. Many people suffer from health defects which the body has become accustomed to bearing without great inconvenience. Such defect sometimes become an aid, rather than a hindrance to development for the simple reason that the individual who has had to learn how to master a bodily handicap, will often find it easier to master the thoughts and emotions.

A GOOD CIRCLE is always held in a clean quiet place which has been well-ventilated. If it is possible, the room should not be used for some hours before the sitting takes place, except perhaps for quiet meditation or the playing of some music. The spirit helpers often come to cleanse the atmosphere of a room before a circle is held, and their work will not be obstructed if the room is kept free of argument and of the thoughts associated with mundane affairs. The comfort of the room is a matter which is governed by individual taste, but it is sensible to remember that it is easier to remain mentally alert while sitting upright on a chair, than it is if one is sunk into the depths of a padded lounge. The aim should be a state of bodily restfulness and mental alertness. All conditions should be adjusted to induce this end. A comfortable room temperature should be maintained (say, about 64 degrees fahrenheit) and strong perfumes of all kinds, as far as possible be excluded. A little thought will show that if a room is too hot or too cold, the body will be uncomfortable and the mind will be occupied in trying to shut off the sense of bodily discomfort. Perfumes have a strong effect upon the physical sense of smell and indirectly affect the emotions. The use of incense is not advisable, because the blending of aromatics which comprise the incense may cause different emotional responses in individual persons. The aim of the circle is unity. Anything which disturbs that unity should be eliminated.

IS THERE anything which the individual member of the circle should do to facilitate the development of mediumship? The answer to the question can only be that a strict control of the appetites prior to sitting will obviously help towards a harmonious state of being: a very light meal, taken about three hours before the sitting, will mean that the stomach is not uncomfortably full. A heavy meal should never be eaten prior to sitting, as this induces sleepiness. An empty stomach may help the mediumship of some people, but it is my experience that the majority of sitters become self-conscious if their stomach begins rumbling, and they find it difficult to detach their thoughts from the feelings of hunger and the expectation of satisfying it. Treat the body as an essential part of the mediumship; do not pamper it, but see that it is comfortable. The demands of the body for alcohol and tobacco should be regulated. It would be good if all smoking and alcoholic drinking is avoided on the day of the circle, in order to facilitate a more harmonious blending with the other sitters. The heavy smoker will find it hard to believe that the smell of tobacco will cling to his clothing, and will scent his breath. Mediums develop a quickening of all their senses, including the sense of smell, and breath from another sitter which is loaded with the smell of tobacco or alcohol can be absolutely nauseating.

Sexual relationships should be regulated, so that the prospective medium does not attend the circle with any sense of exhaustion. These simple rules should be easy to follow. If sitters cannot control the appetites sufficiently to follow them, then they should cease to strive for development. A person who cannot control the appetites of the body will be unfit to control the more subtle powers associated with mediumship.

THE EARLY spiritualists made it a rule to bathe the body and wear clean clothing before they attended their circles. Unfortunately, this is not possible today when numbers of sitters leave their places of business and go straight to their circles. would urge sitters to make

sure that their clothing is comfortable, and upon the day of the circle to see that no tight belts will hamper the breathing, nor yet uncomfortable shoes affect the feet. Small bodily discomforts quickly become accentuated when the psychic power sensitizes the medium. You want to be able to forget the body and turn your thought to other things. The best way to do this is to make the body reasonably comfortable.

There are various ways of beginning the circle. Some start with the singing of a number of hymns, some begin with the study of an extract from a favorite book. Other circles listen to music from a gramophone. The leader will sometimes deliver an extempore prayer; at other circles the leader will use a set prayer. This part is all a matter of individual preference: in the same way that the regulation of lighting is according to the preference of the person in charge of the circle. Direct light falling straight on the eyes of a sitter will not allow the sitter to relax very easily. Subdued lighting is to be preferred to bright light. Darkness is not essential except for the development of special forms of physical mediumship, though even this form of mediumship is produced in some parts of the world in full daylight.

The time has now arrived when the potential medium is seated in the circle and wondering, sometimes a little fearfully, what is going to happen and what he (or she) is upposed to do. The sitter is usually told to relax and quieten the mind. I am constantly being told by sitters that this is a most difficult feat; "As soon as I try to be quiet," they say, "all kinds of thoughts start coming into my mind, and try as I will, I cannot push them out. Why does it happen?"

I THINK that this inrush of thought is nothing different to that which is happening at other times. The difference is simply that *you* have become sensitively aware of what your mind is doing. If you want to control your thoughts, do not make the mistake of trying to create a vacuum in the mind. You know the phrase: "Nature abhors a vacuum?" Many people seem to have the idea that to meditate, or quieten the mind, means to think of nothing. True meditation means thinking of something to the exclusion of all

other things until the mind is saturated with the subject of its meditation. To think of one thing in this meditative way means that a person has to learn how to concentrate. I would therefore advise the new sitter to try to visualize something simple during the time of meditative quietness. Some people find it helpful to visualize a pool of still water: others prefer a cross, or a few words from a hymn. The subject is unimportant except as an aid to the concentration which will lead on to meditation. When the thoughts wander away from the chosen subject, bring them firmly back until the time arrives when you find yourself sitting with your mind like a clear pool, unruffled by any ripples of your own thought.

The habit of training yourself to concentrate can be carried into the common tasks of the daily life. Learn to watch yourself. While you are at work do you suddenly become aware that you are thinking of something which you are anticipating in your home? When you are reading a book do you sometimes find that you have scanned a whole page while you were thinking of your prospective dinner engagement, and then discover you are quite unaware of the contents? Make yourself think of the job in hand, so that you do it really well. Concentrate on one thing at a time, and you will find it much easier to control your mind when you are in the circle.

CHAPTER II

THE AURA

BEFORE YOU can proceed very far with this study of mediumistic development you must accept the fact that every individual person has an aura, because it is largely through this aura that the spirit beings are able to make their influence felt in the physical realm. It would be helpful to all sitters if they could read *The Human Atmosphere,* by Dr. Kilner, as this book gives a lucid description of the aura as examined with the aid of the dicyanin screen*.

My own booklet, *The Mystery of the Human Aura* gives a more general survey of the aura as I have seen it. This book was inspired by ideas imparted by the spirit of Dr. Kilner.

The aura enfolds every person in a subtle sheath, rather as a shell encloses the yolk of the egg. The aura is intended to be protective. It is the part of man which shields him from the curiosity of his fellows, and which should protect him from the influence of spirits who have not yet become highly spiritual. When development takes place, this aura loses its outer firmness. The person becomes somewhat like the egg without its shell. The shell-less egg is still composed of a yolk, surrounded by transparent substance, and the individual still retains the physical frame surrounded by an aura which is tenuous and which can be expanded and contracted at the will of the individual.

The developing medium should endeavor, by an effort of thought, to expand the aura when sitting in circle so that it will blend with the aura of the persons seated on either side. The simplest way of doing this is to feel an affection for the other sitters and to realize that your endeavor is to become part of the whole circle, rather than just an individual wholly concerned with your development. If you are wholly engrossed

*The dicyanin screen became known as the Kilnascreen.

with yourself and your feelings, it is easy to see that your aura will not expand, but will firmly enclose you, just as it will enclose you if you are afraid. It is almost useless for you to seek development if you are frightened of what you may see or hear, because fear causes the aura to contract, and a contracted aura shuts you off from the flow of psychic force which circulates around a well-conducted circle. The motto of all sitters should be "May I be used — if not for my own development, then to help others develop!"

AFTER YOU have been in the circle for a few times you will become aware of a change of feeling. You should find it easy to settle down and be at peace. You should feel the power coming around you, like something very quiet, but strong and protective. This means that your aura has been blended with that of the other sitters, and you are then a *part* of the circle. Sometimes people complain that there are times when they just connot get into this sense of the peace and power of the circle; others say that they do not attain to it until it is nearly time for the circle to finish. "Thoughts keep popping into my head," they complain, "and I just cannot get rid of them. Do you think a bad spirit is trying to stop my development?"

It is very seldom that a bad spirit gets into a properly conducted circle, and so it is very improbable that the cause of restlessness is due to psychic interference. It is more likely that the person does not realize how the aura can absorb the thought forms which all persons constantly create as they live the daily life. "Thoughts are things!" This is a statement of fact which can be verified by any reliable clairvoyant, who "sees" the pictures created by the thoughts of people.

Many clairvoyants say, as Christmastide approaches, that they "see" colored streamers, trees, candles and Christmassy things in the atmosphere. When the late King George V was dying, numerous psychics claimed that they "saw" him as he was dying. It was not strange that they "saw" the dying monarch. As the thoughts of the whole world were centered upon him, it would have been strange had there not been myriads of thought forms impressed into the psychic atomsphere. The sensitive aura of a medium can absorb these thought forms, in the same way that the egg, when deprived of its shell, can absorb impurities from the air.

Thus it is possible that a journey in a crowded train or bus may result in a sensitive absorbing some of the total thought atmosphere of the crowd, with its jumbled thoughts of home, cinema, food, television, "girl" friend and "boy" friend. In the same way, if there has been a contact with people who have been worried or annoyed, the aura may absorb some of their thought emanations, with the result that the medium will feel vaguely disturbed and unable to settle down in the development time.

I HOPE this idea of absorbing other people's thoughts and auric emanations does not sound alarming. I am afraid it is just part of the process of becoming a medium. It is something which every medium has to learn to overcome, and which *you* will overcome as your mediumship develops. A good way of ridding yourself of such undesirable emanations is to go for a very quiet stroll, breathing deeply as you do so, with the idea that you are inbreathing peace and outbreathing all disturbance and disharmony.

If it is possible to do so, wash your hands thoroughly, and splash your eyes and forehead with cool water.

Later, you will be able to close your aura when in crowded places by an effort of will, and thus protect yourself. It is a good thing to endeavor to visualize your aura as firmly encasing you in a protective shell when you are out of your circle, and when your time of sitting draws to an end, and the circle closes, it is always wise to endeavor to contract the aura. To fold it around you is a better simile, though some mediums use the term "closing" the aura.

THE AURA shows every state of thought and feeling; it can therefore, be controlled by thought and feeling. It expands widely. Conversely, feelings of repulsion cause it to contract into a narrow, protective circle. The developing medium should learn how to master the thoughts in such a way that the aura can be controlled at will. If this is not achieved, the medium will find himself (or herself) influenced by other people's moods to such an extent that it will be difficult to discover what moods belong to the medium and which are the ones the aura has absorbed from other people. Some people consider it a sign of good mediumship when a sensitive is registering pains, moods and psychic impressions at all times and in all places. It would be more correct to describe it as uncontrolled mediumship. A medium should be able to reject impressions, as well as to accept them, for from this basis will develop the ability to reject the influence of undesirable spirits, as well as accepting the communications from good ones.

Now let us consider what may happen when you open your aura and blend it with the aura of the other members of the circle. If you are clairvoyant, you will see that some of the auras are stronger and brighter than others. The aura of the leader, or medium in charge of the circle, is generally the most fully developed, and the spirit guides of this leader will endeavor to send through it certain rays, which will flow from aura to aura until the whole group's aura has been circled. In this way the new members of the circle become blended into the aura of the whole group, and the weaker auras become strengthened from the totality of the circulating spiritual force.

When everyone is in good health and a happy frame of mind the power circulates freely, and at the end of the sitting everyone should feel uplifted and invigorated. If one or two members are slightly unwell, then they will absorb some small part of the power, and the whole group may feel slightly invigoration. This does not mean that sitters should refrain from attendance at their circle because they feel slightly unwell; their absence is more likely to affect the circle adversely than the small amount of psychic force which they may absorb. Regular attendance on the part of every sitter is most essential to any successful circle.

In the next installment of this essay, Miss Roberts discusses the Spirits and Trance Control.

FLYING SAUCERS
and the
Contact Enigma

by JEROME CLARK

Although this article was written a few years ago, the current revival in interest in UFOs, and the appearance of some more responsible material upon the question, makes it very timely indeed.

ANYONE WITH sufficient temerity to admit a belief in flying saucers is bound to be asked, sooner or later, what his opinion is regarding stories of landings and subsequent sightings of UFO occupants. Unfortunately, a simple answer to a question of this type is virtually impossible, due to the almost incredible amount of confusion surrounding the subject. The newcomer to the field is in most cases a complete skeptic of all such accounts, taking the view (as this writer did) that no rational person could believe them. However, there are very few individuals of any experience in saucer research who completely discount *every one* of these reported incidents. Aime Michel, by virtue of his discovery of "orthoteny," * has proven conclusively that at least *some* are true. Therefore, the question with which we shall concern ourselves is not *if* they can be believed — only *how much* they can be believed.

There are three basic kinds of UFO occupant reports. The first is the simple sighting with no attempt at any contact or communication; the second, which the writer has termed the "borderline contact," is composed of the sighting and *very limited* communication — such as that evidenced in the famous Papua, New Guinea, affair of 1959, in which an Anglican missionary and a dozen native witnesses exchanged hand signals with the crew of a hovering craft;** and the more "orthodox" contact claim, in which the "contactee" receives long philosophical discourses from

generally benevolent brethren from other planets, is usually effected by radio or mental or physical experience, and is often deliberate, which is not the case with the other two types cited.

Among "UFOlogists", reports of the first variety are almost universally accepted, the second somewhat less so, and the third almost not at all — not, anyway, by the more rational elements in the field. On the surface this attitude seems peculiar, but a deeper examination reveals one very good reason for it: the so-called contactees have never produced any evidence that would convince a three-year old Mongoloid idiot. Perhaps, in fairness, we should revise that statement slightly to say that they have never produced any evidence to substantiate their claims *at face value.* Some researchers, notably Peter Kor, have suggested that there is a certain grain of truth in some of the claims which, as yet, has not been determined.

If someone were taken to another planet or "merely" given

Flying Saucers and the Straight-Line Mystery, Criterion Books, 1958

**Brisbane, Australia, *Sunday Mail,* August 16, 1959.

a jaunt through outer space, it hardly need be said that he would have no trouble at all in proving it. Professor Charles A. Maney, in *The Challenge of Unidentified Flying Objects,* sums up the situation perfectly:

"A very obvious basis by which a contact claimant could establish the truth of his claims would be the securing of some artifact or gadget from extra-terrestrial sources. Or even the submission of some intellectual plan, a new scientific experiment or a new mathematical formula, in fact anything which by test by competent scholars could be shown to be new in this world, would serve to validate the claims of a contactee. Up to the present no evidence of this kind has been presented to competent terrestrial authority. Thus it is that there are few if any investigators of UFO phenomena of scientific background who recognize the claims of the present day crop of contact claimant businessmen."

ONE CONTACTEE has made a vain attempt to answer Professor Maney's challenge. He is George Adamski of California, the original and most vocal of the clan. In his second book, *Inside the Space Ships,* he describes a scene he allegedly witnessed while aboard a Venusian flying saucer, and in so doing uses the term "fireflies" to connote the appearance of the stars against the black background. Seven years later, after American astronaut John H. Glenn, Jr., reported seeing an unexplained phenomenon which he compared to the lights of fireflies, Adamski and his associates cried collectively, "We told you so!" Even ignoring the difference in altitude (Adamski claimed to be about 50,000 miles out and Glenn only 100), we find no convincing similarity, for what Glenn saw were definitely *not* stars. Adamski, realizing this, has apparently attempted to obscure the meaning of his original description.

Not all contacts are as obvious hoaxes as is Adamski's, since in many cases the witnesses appear to be sincere people. Most of these can be safely explained as mere wishful thinking, and a few as rather pathetic cases of sexual repression. In one account, for example, a very plain middle-aged woman describes her seduction by an "extremely handsome" Venusian. Other accounts by other contactees are very obviously fantasies of sick minds.

But to dismiss *all* claims as intentional or unintentional hoaxes would be to beg the question, for there are some which, if more fully investigated, might very well prove true. Unfortunately, these stories lack the necessary details to be adequately corroborated; but if they are not spurious, they could prove to be the long-awaited breakthrough leading to the solution to the UFO mystery itself.

One of these reports was uncovered by Italian researcher, Alberto Fenoglio, in interviews with a number of Soviet citizens, among them a diplomat and an engineer. Some time in 1961, it is claimed, a woman parachutist jumped from an airplane, whose pilot then decided to land and wait for her. However, she did not appear until *three days later* in the town of Saratov, Russia, where she explained that she had been abducted in mid-air by a flying saucer. The ship's three occupants, who are not described in the account, took her for a trip into outer space so to enable her to view Earth from there. The woman brought with her to the city an envelope containing a message for "the authorities", which she gave to the local police chief. Its contents have not been revealed.

Needless to say, if the account is accurate, there is no way in which a hoax could have been perpetrated. This writer prefers to remain slightly skeptical, though, at least until more exact details are forthcoming. UFO students are aware of many irresponsible and fantastic stories that have been circulated during the past seventeen years — so many, in fact, that they should be suspicious of any unusual report which is not fully corroborated. On the other hand, they should not dismiss such accounts only *because* they are fantastic.

ONE PARTICULARLY strong reason for doubting the veracity of a number of contact claims is the fact that many seem to be vehicles through which the claimant espouses his own off-beat political and philosophical ideas. A pertinent example of this would be the late William D. Pelley, who headed an organization dubbed "Soulcraft." Pelley, as some readers are doubtless cognizant, headed the notorious "Silver Shirts" in the pre-War days, an organization dedicated to arousing pro-German sympathies among Americans. (Pelley eventually wound up in prison for his seditious activities, incidentally.) During the '50's' he took advantage of widespread interest in UFOs and related subjects by sporting a contraption that he claimed could contact dead persons, among them Benjamin Franklin, Thomas Jefferson, and Henry Ford; it goes without saying that these individuals came through with viewpoints strangely reminiscent of Pelley's!

We shall now examine the first two types of saucer occupant reports. The first cannot in fairness be called "contact claims", for they do not involve actual communication to any degree; the second, however, are and do, yet at the same time they do not involve long and dreary discourses on extraterrestrial philosophy. As far as any has got is detailed in a report from Everittstown, New Jersey, on November 6, 1957, in which a little man of gnomish appearance asked a startled farmer for his dog. The reply was a simple "Get the hell out of here!" *

Elsewhere the author has set eight requisites of a borderline contact. In order for the reader better to understand the nature of such accounts, they are listed below:

1. The witnesses are usually ordinary people; they are never prepared for a contact.
2. They are puzzled and often annoyed by their experiences.
3. They do not seek publicity or try to profit in any way.
4. The occupants are almost invariably human in appearance, although their sizes may vary.
5. They are friendly or, as in a minority of cases, indifferent to the witnesses.
6. They may speak, but they do not discuss philosophical, economic, or scientific theories.
7. They always have a definite purpose in mind, such as collecting plant, soil or water samples, or perhaps merely communicating with witnesses.
8. They do *not* take witnesses for trips in their craft.

A GOOD EXAMPLE of a case agreeing with each of the

*Milford, New Jersey, *Delaware Valley News*, November 15, 1957.

above eight points allegedly occurred on November 7, 1957, to a truck driver named Malvan Stevens, who, it is said, was driving near House, Mississippi, at 7:25 a.m. (CST) when a large, egg-shaped object landed on the highway in front of him. Two men and a woman, all 4-1/2 feet in height, with dark hair and dressed in gray suits, emerged. They acted friendly and talked to him in a "chattery" tongue, and one of them tried to shake his hand. After a short time they re-entered their craft and flew away.

At first Stevens told his story only to several fellow workers, who in turn passed it on to the Meridian, Mississippi, *Star.* An 8-year old girl residing in House, by way of corroboration, reported that she had seen a "round ball moving through the sky at sunup". Stevens, however, refused publicity, saying, "I'm making myself look like a fool."

Harold T. Wilkins, in his *Flying Saucers on the Attack,* quotes an account sent him by an Oklahoma lady, who writes that "many years ago", while she was traveling through Missouri in a covered wagon, she listened to her father talk to an old frontiersman:

"He was an old man and he told my dad that, about 40 years ago, he, the old man, was a lad and had gone hunting in the hills, where he saw a round thing settle down from the sky on the bald top of a mountain overhead. He was frightened, but that did not stop him from climbing up the mountain to see who it was. 'It stood in the clearing of some woods, and was like a big silver ball.' Soon, a piece of the top slid back and two things came out. Said the old man: "They wuzzn't as tall as me; but sure was nice-lookin' folks. Hadn't much on their purty bodies and legs, that's sure; but the gal wuz as purty as a filly on a medder in the spring a-foolin' round an' raisin' the passions of an old spavined stallion, and then kickin' her heels and dashin' off. They tried to talk to me, but neither of us could understand what the other said. I was too scared to say much. Then they stepped back into the ball, slid back the lid, and the ball went up into the sky till it was lost to my eyes. Yep, it's the doggone truth I'm tellin' yo', though smarties round this location say I alwuz was loco.'"

In line with cases like the above, it is interesting to

note that, according to George Hunt Williamson, the Chippewa Indians of northern Minnesota have a legend of little men who came in "sky boats" to help them develop new methods of planting. Since the advent of the white man, the Chippewas claim the men do not come very much.

The first type of saucer occupant reports concerns little, hairy, dwarf-like creatures that often exhibit vicious characteristics. Neither of the latter two types of contacts is nearly so convincing, nor so widely accepted among investigators, as those of the little men. At first glance these stories appear ridiculous, though even the casual reader may be impressed with the obvious sincerity of the witnesses. (One woman, in fact, told officials of Civilian Saucer Intelligence, New York, that she would give everything she had if she had not experiended her encounter with these creatures.) However, a closer examination reveals a definite pattern in the incidents, particularly in the descriptions of the beings themselves.

What do they look like? Major James R. Randolph, an authority on interplanetary subjects, has described his conception of an inhabitant of the planet Mars, based upon the logical form such life would take under existing conditions: "He has slender arms and legs, a large chest, wide, flaring nostrils and a broad mouth. His head would be a quarter the size of his body; his eyes would be dark-adapted, with wide pupils . . . he would be about four feet tall." *

This description fits almost perfectly that given by witnesses of these mysterious beings.

Of the three types of extraterrestrials reliably reported (little hairy dwarfs, small "people" like those seen by Malvan Stevens, and blond men of Nordic-Oriental appearance and normal size), the first seem to be the least advanced, in that the other two make every effort to *refrain* from violence, while the first make an equal effort to *cause* it.

Coral Lorenzen, director of the Aerial Phenomena Research Organization** and also one

---

*"How Scientists Visualize the *Real* Flying Saucer Men," *Mechanix Illustrated,* June 1951.
**4145 East Desert Place, Tucson, Arizona.

of the most brilliant researchers in the field; suggested recently that the latter two are the true intelligences, whereas the hairy dwarfs are actually moderately intelligent animals somewhat like monkeys. This hypothesis appears most logical and it would explain why, for example, the dwars are hostile particularly when startled and why they are often seen doing the most "menial" tasks, including the collection of soil and water samples.

IN THIS WRITER'S opinion, though, a far more accurate parallel would be modern civilized man as compared to the Neanderthal, since the dwarfs are apparently more trainable than are monkeys. Moreover, they seem to have some kind of working arrangement that requires a certain degree of intelligence, as evidence the incident quoted below. The speaker is an uneducated Brazilian farmer named Olmiro da Costa e Rosa, who lives about two and a half miles from Venancio Aires, Rio Grande do Sul, and who at the time was talking to government investigators:

"On December 9, 1954, at 5:00 p.m., I was mowing in a French-bean and maize field when I heard a strange noise, resembling that of a sewing machine. At the same time, the animals in the nearby pasture ran away hastily. Raising my body, bent over my hoe working on the ground, I saw a stranger. He was very near, just looking at me. Then I also noticed, at a small distance from the place I was, a craft shaped like an explorer's hat. It was a cream color, protected by a kind of transparent smoke, and was not in contact with the ground. The unknown engine was stopped in mid-air, motionless, at about five feet above the ground. A strong smell was coming from it, a smell that can be compared to that of the smoke expelled by steam-locomotives using coal as fuel.

"It was then that I observed, behind that first man, two other human figures: one was inside the craft with his head outside; another was more distant, close to the fence, and apparently doing a careful examination of the barbed-wire. On the top of the craft I saw three holes, but I don't know how the two men came out because I didn't see it, I was so scared. I tried to cry for help, but no sound came from my throat. I couldn't even move my legs to run away, the fear was paralyzing. The hoe fell from my hands.

"The stranger made a greeting gesture, which looked like a military compliment, followed by a sad smile. Afterward, he kneeled down to get the hoe, looked at it from all sides, turning the tool deftly with the hands. After studying it carefully, he gave it to me again, *i.e.*, he placed again the hoe in my hands. Then, he picked up from the soil French-bean and maize plants (he rooted out a sample of each) and, without a word, left toward the craft—apparently no longer interested in my problems.

"Seeing that there was nothing to be feared, I controlled my nerves and walked toward the craft. But my movements were attentively observed by the man who was inside the craft. He was watching me carefully all the time, but did nothing to stop me. But the other, the one who was still at the fence, more distant, made a negative sign toward me—clearly showing that I was not allowed to come closer to the machine. I stopped, of course, and decided to go toward the fence, to see what he was doing there. He was studying the wires with the eyes and fingers, making a careful examination.

"Some sheep that had run away at the beginning were now coming back and approaching the place. I saw that the stranger was looking at them with a great interest. With words and gestures, I asked if he accepted one of them — as a gift. The stranger seemed to understand and answered with a negative sign.

"AFTER THIS, I don't know how to tell, because things happened fast, but they went back to the craft, disappeared inside it — and suddenly I was alone . . . The alien craft took off vertically, climbing up about thirty feet. Then it accelerated brusquely and flashed away obliquely through the sky, at great speed, vanishing toward the west.

"The three men can be described as beings of medium stature, broad-shouldered, blond and with long hair which blew in the wind. The faces were so similar that they might be taken, easily, as twins. They didn't look like normal persons because of their slanted eyes and their pallid faces. The pallor of their skin was so intense, in fact, that their faces looked like those of 'corpses.' They appeared, however, to be strong.

"These strange men were dressed in light brown clothes, which were one-piece garments like overalls, or uniforms. The trousers were close-fitted and seemed to be linked with the shoes. The shoes were odd; they had no heels — the footprints they left in the earth showed this clearly.

"The whole thing lasted approximately five minutes. The alien craft was large and might have, perhaps, a diameter of about 50 feet. It appeared to be made of a yellow metal, very light (in color), and shining brightly (in spite of the yellow color).

"After the take-off, I searched the ground at the area above which the craft was stopped all the time. I found nothing. The smell of burning coal (fossil-coal) remained, for some time, in the air after the craft's departure."

Government investigators were very much impressed with da Costa's story, for he told it to them in a straightforward, simple manner and was obviously sincere. Moreover, the term "flying saucers" meant nothing to him, and he did not read science-fiction because he was only semi-literate. In fact, he expressed the opinion that the visitors were airplane pilots from another country. After carefully studying all possible angles, the officials who took part in the investigation had no choice but to label it "un-explained".

But to compound matters even more, another incident took place exactly two days later, *at 5 p.m.*, the same hour that da Costa's alleged visitation had occurred, this time a mile away on a farm belonging to Pedro Morais.

Morais was planning to go to town to buy food when he heard the frightened squawkings of his chickens, and thinking they were being disturbed by a sparrow-hawk, he went to investigate. On the way, he happened to glance up, and there he spotted an object which he described as resembling "the hood of a jeep, on the top; and like an enormous, polished brass kettle, on the lower part". The UFO was making a noise resembling that of a sewing machine.

It was then that Morais noticed two small, 4-foot figures standing in the field. The farmer, puzzled and annoyed, started advancing toward the creatures to tell them to get off his field; but when ten yards separated him from the nearer one, it held out its hand to signal him to go no further. He did not stop, and the aliens began running toward their ship. Just before it entered, the being nearer the UFO plucked a tobacco plant from the soil; then they were gone.

"The figures were only human in the shape of the head and body," Morais said later in describing them. "All the time, I concentrated my eyes upon their faces, but I didn't see their eyes, the nose, the mouth or the ears. There was nothing of the kind; no face was visible. I got the impression that they were placed in a kind of sack of yellow color, which enveloped their bodies completely, from the head to the feet."

NEITHER OF the two above incidents could be said to be proven, but the similarity is so striking that circumstantial evidence alone makes their veracity very probable. The two farmers, da Costa and Morais, had never met, even though they lived very close together, and neither had heard of UFOs. Each interpreted differently what he saw. (Morais believed his visitors to be "devils.") And neither case has ever been explained, despite thorough investigation carried out by the Brazilian government.

Incidents like the above allow us to draw some rather general conclusions. Da Costa's visitors seem to be the more intelligent, for they engaged in limited contact, whereas Morais's ran when they were approached. Nevertheless, the two sets of extraterrestrials seem to have been on the same basic mission, whatever that may have been — note the time similarity, for example.

If Major Randolph's views are correct, then it is probable that the little men come from Mars. And their taller, more handsome brethren? In the writer's view they probably come from another solar system — explorers who colonized Mars, finding there semi-intelligent creatures they could train for routine missions. They arrived sometime in the early 1870's, setting up two space stations (the so-called Martian moons, *as per* Dr. Webb's theory). Even before then, they had come, but only occasionally. For some reason, however, possibly the advance of terrestrial civilization, they found it necessary to maintain detailed surveillance; since then, they have watched Earth very closely and will undoubtedly continue to do so for many years to come.

REFERENCES

1. *Flying Saucers and the Straight-Line Mystery,* Criterion Books, 1958
2. Brisbane, Australia, *Sunday Mail,* August 16, 1959.
3. Milford, New Jersey, *Delaware Valley News,* November 15, 1957.
4. "How Scientists Visualize the *Real* Flying Saucer Men," *Mechanix Illustrated,* June 1951.
5. 4145 East Desert Place, Tucson, Arizona.

The Great Exile

by JACK WILLIS

(author of *The Way of Dreams, The Great Breath*)

"MOMMA, HOW did I get here?" asks the child. Mother knows how, of course but how can she answer? The birds and the bees have been worn out, long ago in our present sophisticated society. Mother now turns to religion and says, "God made you and put you here". That answer satisfies the child for too short a time and then the inevitable, "Momma — why did God make me and put me here?" Mother would now be out on a limb, but she is prepared since the first question. "Because God loves you and wants you to be happy." That interests the child and now he is also prepared and wants to know "Why God loves him? "'Why" God put him here? and "Why" God wants him to be happy?

So the questions go on and on, into maturity, old age and right up to death. Those questions are seldom properly answered, to our satisfaction, for most of us. I have read of great men with great minds, going from religion to religion, philosophy to philosophy and still arriving at the moment of departure in a state of uncertainty.

Uncertainty is a frightful state of mind to be in when one is facing the unknown. It embraces hesitation, suspense, illusion, fear and terror. These are untrustworthy traveling companions to have with you when you are seemingly propelled into an unknown dimension, across the River Styx.

The River Styx is not really the River of Death. It is only

mythological, and could just as well be the River of Rebirth. When we die here on Earth, we are released from The Great Exile, for Earthlife in our physical body is imprisonment for the soul, just as surely as if it were exiled from its own true state of being. If you were exiled into unfriendly, unhappy surroundings, foreign to your nature, wouldn't you feel imprisoned? Imprisonment and exile are, to the higher planes of consciousness, similar to temporary death, although death is only an illusion.

The true state of being is surely not in the physical body. It must be, therefore, the spiritual soul that carries the indestructible Spark of God that possesses immortal life. Both *The Great Breath** and *The Great Exile* are my interpretations of Theosophical Teachings.

The Spiritual Soul is the source of life to the physical body. As the mind is to the human brain, and as electricity is to an automobile's magneto, so the life is the Spark of God, is the source of life to our Spiritual Soul. Without life, there could be no function, from atom to galaxy. As God's Spirit in our Souls must have an insulation or vehicle in our Spirit, so our Spirit must have insulations or vehicles in which to manifest itself in our three-dimensional and five-sensed Earth world.

God's Spirit permeates all time, space, and substance, manifesting as life and intelligence by way of the mind through the physical brain, from the most progressed human being to the lowest existing amoeba. Spirit penetrates the cosmos in magnetic and anti-magnetic rays that carry and produce powers that are unknowable to us. Our brains are the vehicles for the mind; mind is the vehicle for thought; thought is the vehicle for desire; desire is the vehicle for our Spirit; our Spirit is the vehicle for God's Spirit; God's Spirit is the vehicle for God's consciousness and God's consciousness is the power by which God breathes on and on in The Great Breath, "asleep" or "awake". Our life Consciousness is that Life Power in the physical vehicles in which we live that

*EXPLORING THE UNKNOWN, July and September 1965.

keeps our physical bodies alive, by the use of our parasympathetic nervous systems, so that we too, subconsciously breathe on and on, asleep or awake.

The vibratory rate of God's Spirit is beyond our conception. It must be insulated with vehicle within vehicles as a high-powered wire must be covered with many layers of insulations before it can be handled.

God's Spirit in the nucleus of the human Soul is comparable, in the most extreme ratio, to the electricity in that wire.

IT IS THE familiar pattern, as I explained in *The Great Breath,* about cells within cells and galaxies within galaxies. I tried to establish an acceptance of the belief in the existence of God's intelligence manifesting from the greatest creation in the macrocosm to the most sub-microscopic reaction in the microcosm. If correct then it certainly manifests itself, in the nucleus of our human souls.

The Nucleus is called the Atma. It has six insulations, vehicles or bodies. The Buddi is the insulation, or vehicle, or body for The Manus—which is a duality called The Lower and Higher Manus (Manus means Mind); it is the insulator, vehicle, or body for the Buddhi that carries the Atma. The Lower and Higher Manus is the individualized human Soul. It has four insulations, vehicles, or bodies. Now you have the complete picture of the immortal human Soul. The indestructible Atom or Spark of God called the Atma, with its two principles, one, two, and three called The Atma—Buddhi—Manus, make the Divine Trinity known in Christianity as The Father, The Son, and the Holy Ghost: The same "threads" by different names.

Now we come to the Seven Principles of the Human Body. The Soul (The first three principles, one, two, and three called The Atma—Buddhi—Manus) must have insulations, vehicles, or bodies to slow it down from the high spiritual vibrations of the higher spiritual planes of consciousness. It makes use of three more progressively grosser bodies of semi-physical or protoplasmic substance in order to manifest itself in the human physical body without injury to the human body, as the physical body could not withstand the vibratory rate of the Soul. So the Soul—one two and three—

takes on the Casual or Desire body, number four; then the Astral body, number five; then the Ethereal body, number six; then at last, it is ready to enter the Physical body, number seven.

Here we must jump the three intermediate bodies, four, five and six, from the Soul as one, two, and three to the physical body number seven. We will try to show how the Soul gets into, and out of, the physical body by way of the proto-plasmic bodies four, five, and six.

When the Soul, the incoming Entity, by the laws of Karma and Dharma (Debt and Duty) has selected "Its" parents, or instruments through which "It" will manifest "Itself" in an in-carnation, strange things begin to happen. As if by a miracle the selected mother and father are brought together and the selected mother is "wedded, bed-ded, and impregnated". If the parents are already married and have children, it may be the magnetic attraction of the family Group that attracts this partic-ular Entity from past associa-tions in past lives. Miraculous escapes of the father, as in war, have been recorded before con-ception and subsequent death that followed soon after. "His luck ran out", "His number came up", His time had come", has been said by his buddies. There are many miracles before the predestined birth, that, in itself, is a miracle.

The whole seven potential principles are brought together at conception by the miraculous conjunction of two separate, human microscopular, male and female, unicellular organ-isms (physically mentally and spiritually carrying cells, within cells), all carrying the blue-prints for specific reproductions, (to be supplied by the mother) of the complete protoplasmic and physical human being as a galaxy of cells, within a galaxy of cells. These seven principles are now miraculously held to-gether until the death of the physical body.

At the moment of death, the first six principles leave the physical body, number seven, as one body, but begin to sepa-rate immediately afterward. The Soul carrying the first three principles, separates from, or sheds the three protoplasmic in-sulations "It" had to take on to get into the physical human body. So, the physical death is spiritual rebirth, for "It" gravitates to "Its" own plane of consciousness.

Here is where death simulates birth, as birth simulates death. As the Soul sheds the three instruments of "Its" imprisonment in the physical body at death, so does the baby shed its three instruments of imprisonment in its mother's physical body, at birth, by shedding first, the Uterus, second, the Amniotic sac, and third, the amniotic fluid.

THE PRIMARY reason of "Why" we are here, is to gain experience and to learn, though the grosser vibrations of physical matter, the lessons we failed to learn, if we have retrogressed. If we are on the way up in evolution, then these are our primary grades through which all must pass in our first corrective studies of human Earthlife. So the Soul must give the physical body the power of life, only by which "It" could function in the human body. If the Soul lives a full Earth-lifetime in the human body "It" can learn lessons of experience that are more subject to impressions, in substance, than "It" could learn in Spirit; for in Spirit "It" learns the lessons of a higher consciousness. So we learn through lessons of experience as a child learning

to walk and being subjected to the treatment received by the human body. To know every human emotion from the lowest physical sensation to the highest spiritual illumination and to learn to know "The Real" from "The Unreal". It may take many Earthlives, for on the upward road of evolution and by progression "It" will have learned many lessons the hard way before "It" begins to learn the easy way — as from past experience or from instructive memory. "It" will know or will have known all desires, by evolving through Earthlife. Dreams and reality; pain and pleasure; the agonies of success and failure, joy and remorse, hunger, thirst, and luxury, love, anger, hate, and lust, will all have taken their tolls here in Earthlife. At Earthdeath, is "It" not "reborn" and freed to gravitate up to, or down to, "Its" own normal plane of consciousness, in progression or retrogression that "It" has earned for "Itself" through millions of "rebirths" in and out of the Great Exile? So you see, there really is no death; it is ever and always a Rebirth.

IT MAY BE a Heaven or a Hell consciousness to which one

gravitates, depending upon one's own progression. If death and birth are identical, why then should we rush from one to the other, either by coming into or going out of Earthlife? Rushing out of Earthlife in suicide has caused much discussion; and committed here on Earth, this act releases the Soul only temporarily, for Suicides must reincarnate soon again on Earth at a lower level of opportunities because of their previous failure. There is no chance to prepare themselves spiritually in that lower plane of remorseful consciousness to which they descend after suicide; so they return, retrogressed, and in a lower state of confident ability than they were before. Victims of early death—by accident, war, murder, or criminal execution—usually reincarnate sooner than they would have reincarnated, if they had been permitted to remain imprisoned in the physical body, subjected to the double imprisonment of the mental punishment of remorse, fear, and the lessons of Life that might have penetrated the shells of illusion that insulate their Souls. These retrogressed or unprogressed Souls carry the scars of their previous life and death, physically, mentally, morally, emotionally, and spiritually. These scars of "Karma" and "Dharma"—unpaid Debt and Undone Duty, usually referred to as "Debt and Duty"—are understood in the West as the unwritten laws of Retributive Justice.

As we kill our enemies and execute our criminals to get rid of their unwanted bodies, we only release their sick, unprogressed Souls to reincarnate again, drawing back into themselves the same weak, vicious personalities and characteristics, with the same ambitions, desires, greeds, fears, and hates that destroyed them before. But this time they have less intelligent control, because of their past retrogression; and so they return with less ability to face successfully, the same situations —and also, perhaps, the same reincarnated Souls that stopped them in their previous failure. It is a credit to fail if one is trying hard to accomplish an altruistic goal that is too great to reach in this incarnation; but it is a failure to succeed if the goal is selfish greed and self-aggrandizement at the expense and suffering of other human beings. This might even include our treatment of the animal kingdoms, but I would be criticizing the work of our experimenting biological scientists, who claim humanitarianism.*

These heavily laden "Karmic" and "Dharmic" Souls reincarnate soon again, as the suicides and executed murderers do, ferrying back and forth between Earth and spirit states of Hell consciousness, reliving in memory and in dream re-enactments the same tragedies, crimes, suffering, thrills, fears, remorse, and violent deaths over and over, never really getting a chance to rest and plan a better life. Remorse is a great affliction and often drives people insane and to suicide. It also teaches severe lessons and *often saves a Soul from further retrogression.***

A HUMAN BODY without the life essence may not be as "dead" as we think; the cells and molecules separate, decompose, dissolve, and disappear from the state of existence in the grossness of matter as we know it. To what extent they go in dissolution we may not realize, beyond a spoonful of ashes for the cremated human body. Perhaps they, too, have some subtle form of "souls" that continue to "be" in a higher dimension of potential future existence, all their own. If so, then they are not dead. They have only been reconverted back (or forward) to their original state of "being", carrying with them the spiritual blueprints, or scandas, of their original characteristics, from their previous exist-

*Other writers on reincarnation do not hesitate to stress this point. RAWL.

**Despite the negative conditions, Light is still there; there are still opportunities for the retrogressed soul to see and respond to the Light, thus starting to progress again. An analogy can be made to a person justly convicted and sent to prison who "learns" from this experience and emerges a "new" person who thereafter is a credit to society. The analogy breaks down when we consider that human punishment is often cruel and vindictive and often does not offer fair opportunities for the convict to learn the lesson the prison is supposed to teach. God's Laws are perfect and are Perfect Love, never punishment, never vindictive. If this were not so, then reincarnation doctrine would be as cruel as those doctrines that depict God torturing people forever because of their failures, "sins", etc., in the course of one short Earthlife. RAWL

ence in Earthlife substance. Their dissolution is by the process of nature's laws of decomposition into their elemental, invisible, molecular structure, known to us a potential energy.

Perhaps these scandas are the spiritual potential genes in the physical cells that carry the spiritual blueprints for the reproduction of the whole cell. I hope this adequately dispenses with the subject of what happens to the physical human body when we die — which is not death, but reconversion.

Now number six, the vehicle for the physical body, is the Ethereal body, which is the life essence of the physical body. As the electric spark from the spark plug ignites the gas in the combustion chamber, moving the cylinder of an automobile and giving it the ability to move, so does the Ethereal body carry the life essence to give the physical body the power to move. When the physical body dies and the Ethereal body slips out of the physical body, it is called the Ethereal shell. It is the ghost-like, transparent little cloud that is seen, by Sensitives, to leave the physical body at the exact moment of death, severing the elastic, electro-magnetic silver cord by which, it was held in the physical body.

It is seen as an aura of a live person and is used in diagnosis by those Psychics or Sensitives who can tell whether a sick person will live or die. It starts to slip out of the physical body before death and the diagnosis is determined by its position in the physical body. It is often Earthbound after it leaves the physical body in death. It sometimes can't understand that it does not have a physical body any more, in which to express itself on the physical plane. Only Sensitives can see it; so, as most people can't see it, they ignore it. If they could, they would most certainly become frightened. It walks right through people, buildings and all Earth substance and may become panic stricken. Can you imagine a frightened ghost? It sometimes causes much trouble haunting the place of its departure from the physical body, especially if its departure was caused by accident or murder. In its hauntings, it sometimes becomes a mischievous ghost called a Poltergeist and really seems to enjoy frightening and annoying people. Ghost stories have long been a drug on the literary market, but Danton Walker's, *Spooks Deluxe,* is a gold mine of authenticity, and *Unbidden Guests* by Wms. Stevens is an atomic bomb that should destroy all of your doubts.

This ghostly shell of a once-living person, retains the appearance of the original person; its personality and characteristics are the same. It sometimes carries the power of repossession, called possession of a weak-charactered, living person.

It may be the evil shell of an evil person that takes posession of a mentally weak person and makes that weak living person do the will of the discarnate evil person. Dope addicts, drunkards, imbeciles, or the mentally retarded, are perfect vehicles for an evil shell to possess and use, to fulfill the evil desires of the dead one.

But the influence could be a good and beneficent one, emanating from the shell of a loved one, or a loving friend, who would inspire to create by helping the lesser person do greater things or to finish the work left undone, at the death of the person whose shell is doing the influencing.

I once read of a great artist, whose works were highly valuable influencing after death, a friend of lesser ability to create valuable masterpieces that were as great as his own.

Warnings have been known, to have been given by the shell of a dead friend, in the dreams of a live man that saved the dreamer's life twenty years after the dream. The shell of a loving friend would be a friend; the shell of an enemy would be an enemy. A complete stranger of weak and evil character could be easily used by an evil shell to commit terrible crimes and cause great sorrow on Earth before the shell would disintegrate, fade, and disappear into the great reservoir of reserve ethereal matter, to be used again when needed to recreate the ethereal body of its original, evil reincarnating entity.

An ethereal shell's power for good or evil depends upon the good or evil power carried by the person when alive in a human body. A good altruistic, spiritual, and intelligent person could not leave an evil shell. So why be afraid of the ghost of a loved one, who is trying to help or to warn in some way? (Or perhaps, it is in need of an explanation of it's own condition.)

NOW, THE fifth principle, known as the Astral body: It is less gross than the Ethereal body and it is the one in which we travel, in our dreams, when we are asleep and sometimes dream a prophetic dream.

During a prophetic dream, the sleeping physical body, completely permeated with its life essence the Ethereal body, remains in bed, but connected with the Astral body by the magnetic silver cord that is strong and elastic all during life and breaks only at death. While the physical body rests in sleep the Ethereal body must stay with the physical body, as the life essence, to preserve the subconsical body.

If the physical body is attached to one end of the silver core, the other end of the silver cord must be attached to the Soul; for after all, the important point is that this is the incarnation of the Soul. So, in a prophetic dream, the Soul and its vehicle, the Desire body, all in the Astral body, jet out of the physical body on mind power, with the speed of thought, to the dream locality on the dreamers lifeline in the Divine Records known as The Great *AKASHA*.

Space and time do not exist in The Akasha, so wherever in Earth time and space, Earth reality may be, the dreamer is there and reviews a dream rehearsal of a future reality on his own lifeline, extending into the future, at least to the end of this incarnation. I do not know, whether or not it is possible to pick up, in a dream, the future lifeline of a future incarnation; but I do believe from reports, and perhaps from one of my own dreams, that I might have made contact with a past lifeline from a previous incarnation. I shall never forget the sensation of the electric currents that flowed through my physical body as my dream consciousness penetrated the magnetic field of a higher dimension. It was like grasping an electric charged wire.

I did not tell you about this dream in *The Way of Dreams,* as that was not the place for it, but this is the place for it.

I was a young man, a farmer, (locality unrevealed) living with my mother, several sisters, and, I think, one brother. I had a dream mind's consciousness of the farmhouse with large rooms and many beds, and several sheds or barns with their respective yards enclosing cattle, horses, pigs, chickens, turkeys, and ducks.

I was sitting in the living room with my family when my mother arose and walked across the room in front of me going into her bedroom. She gave me the most tender and painful look as she passed me. I interpreted her look with dream telepathy that permits the dreamer to know the true facts of a situation without knowing how or why he knows. I knew she was sick and I was worried about her health. (It was the painful look of suffering and farewell that I've seen in the eyes of my aged mother of this incarnation.)

I followed her into her bedroom; she was lying fully clothed on the bed. I sat down on the edge of the bed and asked her, "How do you feel?" She didn't get a chance to answer, for all the animals and fowl in the barns and the years in back of the house, started screaming in fear, at the tops of their voices. It was animal hysteria, as if a demon were in their midst. Again I knew, as one knows in a dream, that only a phantom or an apparition could cause such a fear reaction among the animals.

I turned from facing my mother to look out through two large french doors that stood wide open by swinging back into the room and against the wall. Several steps led down from the house to a stone-slabbed pathway that lead out to the barn door. The pathway was lined with fruit trees, whose limbs were bare as in early fall. A large full moon in a starless sky sent out the brightest moonlight I had ever seen and there, in the bright moonlight, at the end of the pathway, in front of the barn doors, stood a large, transparent ghost in the form of a woman dressed in quaker clothes. Her dress was dark, her cape was light. It flapped, as if in a breeze, but there was no breeze. Her white bonnet shadowed the face that was not transparent but blanked out as in a photograph. She stood still, with, her transparent hands folded in front of her. She was looking at me through the doors and I was not afraid; but the electric charges that flashed through my body seemed to reach the point of exploding. I knew, as if being told through the inner ear by a silent voice or like reading the words: "God's Angel of Death has come for my mother."

I turned back to my mother as she started to move to see what it was. I took her in my arms and said, "No, No, don't look." I was then aware that all was silent; not a sound came from the barnyards. As my mother struggled to see the apparition through the open doors behind me, I realized she was a thin, wrinkled and shriveled-up old woman. Then she saw it —and immediately turned into a young woman in the full bloom of health and strength; then she vanished, completely **disappearing** from my sight and my arms. In my dream consciousness, I realized I had seen the death and rebirth of my mother.

I then turned to see the apparition; yes—it was still there. It advanced toward me. It did not walk; it glided, floated with its feet on the ground and its head in the bare tree limbs that passed right through its head like shadows through light. As it advanced a couple of yards, the electric vibrations in my body accelerated; then the apparition stopped, and the vibrations slowed down. It advanced and stopped; each time the vibrations accelerated, then slowed down until it seemed I could withstand the electric charge with it standing before me within arm's length. I found myself standing on the ground in front

of it before the house steps. I reached out my right hand to touch its transparent folded hands, so close to me, but it glided back about a step, as if to tell me not to touch it. I looked close into its face but it had no face; it was still blanked out. Its garments continued to flap gently as if in a breeze, but still there was no breeze. We were alone, just "It" and I. It did not speak; then slowly it began to dissolve and disappeared, vanishing before my eyes just as I've seen steam vanish in the air on a cold day.

AS I AWAKENED I was more physically aware, on the Earth plane of consciousness, of the high velocity of electric vibrations than I had been in the higher dimension of the astral plane.

Every muscle in my body seemed to be on fire and about to explode. As I slowly came back to Earth consciousness in awakening, the vibrations slowed down—as they had in the dream when the apparition stopped on the pathway, as if it knew what was happening to me. After becoming sure I was completely awake I began reviewing the dream from start to finish; and each time the mental

picture of the advancing apparition came on my screen of
thought, the electric vibrations
returned, accelerated, and slowed down, accelerated and slowed
down in exact relationship, as
in the dream.

I violently oppose the interpretation of any dream by anyone else but the dreamer. I
believe the dreamer, and only
the dreamer, can interpret his
dream in accuracy if the dream
is a prophetic dream.

Here is my interpretation of
my own dream. The woman
that was my dream mother, I
knew in this life in which she
was short and plump; in the
dream she was tall and thin.
There were certain wrinkles at
the outside corner of her eyes,
certain features of their faces
that were so similar that identity
could not be denied. The woman
of this life, I loved only in a
platonic friendship as I admired
her and respected her very much
on the mental and spiritual
plane of thought. I knew her in
Florida, when I was in business
here. I had the dream several
months after I left Florida and
had returned to New York City.
We were not destined to be
lovers in this life for my destiny
lay with that of another woman
across the Atlantic Ocean. (I
met her two years after the
dream and married a year after
that meeting.)

I am the only one in the
world to whom the dream is
important. My friend didn't believe in reincarnation; so she
couldn't believe, through our
correspondence, that she could
have been my mother in a previous incarnation. She was tied
too closely to her church teachings and thought that I was
getting to be just a little crazy
in the head. Who but myself
can believe she was my mother
in a previous life, and that my
dream was an illumination —
the benefit of which, as yet, I
do not know?

If a dream is remembered by
the conscious mind it can benefit the dreamer, especially if it
is a warning to save the
dreamer, a friend, or a loved
one, from adversity or destruction; it then depends on the
dreamer's self will, progression,
intelligence, and belief in his
own dream. You should recognize a prophetic dream when
you awaken and if you laugh
at it, ignore the warning, and
forget it, then it is your own
loss. Your own destiny, or that
of the others of the dream, may
be sealed by your own neglect;
so the value you lost would be
something you would learn too
late.

WHEN THE physical body

dies, sometimes the ethereal and astral shells cling together and hang around on Earth many years before disintegrating; a few victims of murder and death by torture during the Middle Ages are still haunting their places of departure, re-enacting, over and over, the terrible crimse that were committed against them. It is thought they are trying to tell us what actually happened and to expose erroneous reports of history. The tenacious courage of a Soul that could make a dying man spit in the face of his torturer, would certainly linger in his shells and give them a stronger and longer life on Earth, long after the Soul had been so hideously ripped from the human body.

Earthbound shells may influence the living beings in many ways. Certain animal pets — especially dogs, cats, and horses — are believed to be able to see them. A dog may continue the daily performance of meeting its master at the door long after the master is dead, acting as if it really sees its master, until the dog finally dies, apparently of no reason, except self will. Shells may inspire artists, writers, musicians, or anyone else in their line of work to do greater things. They may come through dreams or appear as spirits of loved ones at seances.

Remember, they are not the true spirits; they are only the protoplasmic bodies of insulations o the Soul, still carrying the scandas, as personality anc characteristics essences, by the materialization of the shell o the original person. There are even different grades or planes of what we think is Spirit. The Spirit of the ethereal shell is a lower grade or quality than the astral shell, being more gross and closer to material substance as the astral is lower than the causal or desire body. And, of course, as the desire body cannot be compared with the Soul, nor be compared to God, even though the Soul carries the Atma and the Buddhi.

The lower shells retain intelligence and memory and car truthfully lead or mislead the percipient, depending upon the quality of the association between the person, and the person of the shell during Earthlife and also the true spiritual relationship between the entities in previous lives.

These ethereal and astra shells are often erroneously called Earthbound Souls o Spirits, but being only shells in the process of dying like a hu man body is dying on a death bed. Being duplicates of the human body they are disinte grating in proportion to the dis ntegration of the corpse in the grave.

This is a technical point to lear. Ghosts still appear of people whose physical bodies have been completely destroyed by fire, or have been dead so long that their physical bodies are completely dissolved, along with the dissolution of both thereal and astral shells leaving he causal, Fourth or Desire body. The desire to tell the ruth about their death, or to inish unfinished work, is so trong that their Desire Body is till Earthbound.

It has been said that the deposed English king, Edward II, till cries out — in the middle of he night, in the basement of the astle in which he died on September 21, 1327 — that he was murdered and did not die naturally as it was thought at irst. You will find an account of his murder in chapter eleven of *The Three Edwards,* by Thomas Costain; and many historians are convinced that he was indeed murdered. ("Foully lain", to use a phrase of Sir Winston Churchill, for the manner of his murder was most oul indeed.)

Patience Worth's desire consciousness to finish writing her oetry and novels was so strong that she finally came through an amanuensis by the name of Mrs. Pearl Curran, some three hundred years after Patience was killed in an Indian Massacre at Cape Cod, Massachusetts. These are outstanding examples of the power of the Desire or Causal body.

The grotesque ghosts, in partial decay, that are seen by some Sensitives, ghosts hovering over their graves, are very good reasons for cremation, which releases not only the scandas of the physical body, but also the ethereal and astral shells, thus freeing the causal body, so that all are then free to return to their own planes of potential energy.

Ethereal, astral, or even desire shells might hang around the place of the accident or murder, in which, they lost their physical body, as in a dream, still disbelieving they have no physical body to return to.

Such a place, is the highway between St. Petersburg and Tampa, Florida. It is the St. Petersburg side where an old beachcomber was killed by a car years ago. I was personally told by a Sensitive, that she saw the car, in which she had been riding, pass right through the "ghost", and that other people too, had seen it at the same place she saw it, which was near the spot that the beachcomber was killed. It walks along the highway with a fishing pole over its shoulder, evidently being hit over and over again, refusing to be dead.

As the ethereal shell fades away into the ethereal plane, the astral shell is free, lingers on, but eventually fades into the astral plane, freeing the Desire body or Fourth Principle.

The Fourth, causal or Desire, body is reborn again. This Fourth principle is a very important piece of mechanism, with very complex functions; it is "in control of operations" of the human physical bodies in which it must live during the Earth-life exiles of the incarnated Entity. It is the pilot, the driver, or the captain of the other three grosser vehicles of substance, the astral, ehtereal and physical.

It is the center of the balances between the Atma-Buddhi-Manus on the spirit side, and Astral — Ethereal — Physical on the side of matter. It is similar, in some respects, to the parasympathetic nervous system that bridges the chasm between the conscious and subconscious functions of the physical body. Psychic powers come through the Desire body to the subconscious and parasympathetic by way of the pineal gland, located just above the pituitary gland in center of the human head. Sometimes the psychic function of the pineal gland causes a

tickling sensation to be felt i the top center of the head, whe one is receiving inspirationa help from metaphysical source

Don't mistake a sensatio from a physical source as bein valid evidence. You must firs discount *all* physical sources – an insect, a breeze, a drop c water, perspiration or a spec of dust — anything that coul physically cause it. A valid in spiration or message coming from a discarnate Entity, be i guide, teacher, family, friend or loved one, could be picked u by the hairlike antenne on th peneal gland and transmitte from the pineal to pituitary b way of the parasympathetic t the sympathetic nervous systen and on to the conscious mind and physical brain as an actua thought. The receiver's eyes firs open wide; then he claps his hands, scratches the top of hi tickling head, smiles, and says "Why, of course, that is th answer," And, naturally, h thinks that he thought of it him self, with that sponge in his hea he calls a brain.

The Desire body — or rathe the Desire mind — manifest from an important plane of cor sciousness called *KAMALOK.* — The Desire Place, also calle the Desire Plane. There are a many levels in the Desire plan as there are grades of desi that need storage. There are t higher levels for the high desires and the lower levels for the low desires — they are called Upper and Lower Kamaloka. It is the source of man's will power that has been given to him by God. As the Soul enters matter it picks up the scandas of its own desires from past lives — both good and evil — carrying them through to the human subconscious. It is the main office, through which comes all of man's creative thinking. It is strange that Desires are usually classified as evil. Why? A Desire may be as good as it may be evil, whether it is to rob a bank or build an orphanage. However, there are mistakes that may be made; a good, normal, altruistic desire may leave the desire office as a message, a suggestion, a hint or an actual order with no particular instruction of procedure. Procedure is a freedom left to the Will Power of the individual. Then, by the time the desire has gone through the Astral Department, the Ethereal Office, and the Physical execution by the conscious human brain, by voice or physical action, it may be so garbled and distorted on delivery that it would be denied by the home office.

The progression of the individual soul is the influence that stimulates the desire. The desires of highly progressed souls, produce great works for the benefit and progress of humanity, while the desires of unprogressed or retrogressed Souls, retard the progress that would benefit humanity.

HUMAN LIFE on Earth is a preparatory school to which younger, unprogressed Souls gravitate on their upward road of progression out of the animal group Souls. The beginning of our human individualization started about eighteen million years ago, so we have been told, when man first appeared on Earth. When a Soul has reached that point in evolution and has become individualized as a human being, it cannot retrogress back into the animal Group Soul. (Perhaps the animals won't take it.) Once a human always a human, meaning not less than a human at least for the duration of the remainder of this manvantara which is the duration of one complete breath of God. So, in the East it is called a manvantara (completely explained in *The Great Breath*) and to have returned to human life, on this Earth, in this manvantara, is the "Hell" to which the older Souls returned, when they failed to graduate from this planet in the last Manvantara. They are our world leaders with whom we, the younger Souls, find so much fault. We criticize their altruism as weakness; we fear their strength that may become uncontrolled; we seek to receive love, when it should be given. We form opinions before we know any facts. We are cruel little children, learning only from personal experience.

Earthlife in the human body is really a kindergarten in comparison to the higher colleges of the greater planets and certainly a "Hell world" compared to the "Heaven worlds" in the greater galaxies. But perhaps they have their various grades of schools and colleges, the same as we do.

We are the victims of our own self-persecution and justice, in our little Earth world and really haven't progressed very much, spiritually, in relationship to our mental and scientific progress. Lower Kamaloka (lower desires) seems to continue to be the main source of our creative influence.

By now in brief review, we should be well acquainted with our own Seven Principles —

Bodies or Selves — and how our Souls reincarnate. Each principle is insulated by the next in line, as our Souls enter three successively grosser protoplasmic vehicles, in order to slow down the Soul's electro-vibratory rate so that it can manifest in the physical substance of our human bodies. Each insulation becomes the vehicle of the interring principle and the passenger principles that it is carrying. In reverse, at death, each of the lower four principles are shed in succession, releasing each successive imprisoned principle.

We must also be aware that each incoming principle carries its own reconverted appearance, abilities, weaknesses, characteristics, ambitions, unpaid debts and undone duties that have been earned, created or contracted for by ourselves alone in past lives.

We cannot blame others for our weaknesses or failures, nor can we give others credit for our strengths and natural abilities. A "natural" singer, actor, artist or technician of any kind is usually better than a merely trained one and is always easier to work with; such persons have reincarnated knowledge and awareness that even sharpens a newly-acquired ability. "He's a natural", or "She's a natural", is the greatest praise that a coach or teacher can give a student. But note that even the "naturals" need training.

DEVAS are teachers and the *DEVACON* is the land of the teachers. It is the "heaven world", or a higher dimension above the Kamaloka.

We are told that we carry over from life to death only ten percent of our past "Debt and Duty". Any more than that would sink us temporarily, stop our payments and arrest our progression. Even the Souls of Our Wise Ones — including our "saviours" — were not free; even though they carried the Christ consciousness, they were still evolving. (Some have thought that Jesus may have been carrying the reincarnated soul of The Buddha.)

In the payment of our "Debts and Duties", we progress. If we fail to progress, then we remain on the same level and reincarnate over and over, slaves of our own stupid lethargy. If we add more Karma (accumulate greater debts) then we retrogress, sinking lower and lower from Earthlife to Earthlife, until we are back in a human vehicle carrying the scandas of

human savages. Such evil "old ones" retrogressing, and younger ones just starting often meet and make the perfect companions for crime, lust, revenge, rape, and murder, etc. How else but in this way can the young teen-aged human savages that roam our streets and haunt our lives be explained?

These young Souls are the latest to come into human life, by individualization. They need much attention and training as young animals do that have great potential capabilities — if they can be "broken in" and trained to civilized standards. Individualization is the point of no return, since they cannot go back into the group soul from which they come. They may be young souls, or old souls that never progressed; nevertheless, we are harnassed with them. Once a wise, old "evil one" gets a young, ignorant and evil one under his influence, it is not long in Earthtime before the young one is wise in the ways of the old one.

The Retributive Laws of Justice, in the Akasha, are inviolate. Many seemingly "escape" the penalties of human laws and methods of supposed "justice", but never can one escape in the Laws of the Akasha. The

Akasha is supposed to hold the records of the past, from the beginning of this manvantura —and probably, also, the future, for the remainder of it.

We are taught to take one step at a time, or "one life at a time"; but with an awakened awareness of future lives to come, the levels of which will be earned in our present lives, as the level of this life was earned in our past lives. "The Great Exile" is not just one life, however long or short that life may be; it is the sum total of all the lives we will have spent on Earth, irrespective of how many manvanturas it takes us to graduate and evolve into a higher expression of consciousness in God's manifestation in future manvanturas.

The Cogitator's Corner

ALTHOUGH THIS is being written during the first days of August, this cogitator's thoughts are going both backward and forward — forward to the season during which it will appear on the stands, backward to the same season and the things which caught the eye and imagination at the time.

Christmas, Hannukah, St. Nicholas day on December 5th in the Lowlands, Ephifany in Italy, during this time of year each group, in the Northern Hemisphere, celebrates, with some religious festival, the turn of the year, the passing of the longest night and the beginning of longer days. The Jews call it the "Feast of Lights"; the Christians the birth of the Prince of Peace, the Light of the World; always, everywhere, a time for giving, particularly a time for gifts to children.

Here in America. the advertis-ing gets wilder and the idea of light and enlightenment seem to recede into the distance in inverse proportion to the number of potentially lethal (or at least lethal in idea) objects sold; and **it was with a shock last year that the writer picked up a well known mail order catalog and found seven pages devoted to guns as suitable gifts to children for the birthday of the Prince of Peace. This was just guns; it** did not include something over 40 pages of toy soldiers, aviators, war games, imitation hand grenades, and assorted pieces of war equipment such as tanks, cannon, guided missiles (which actually can be guided), instructions on how to make bombs, and the "best" ways of "wiping out the enemy", all **to celebrate the birth of the Prince of Peace.**

The suggestions for adults (male adults, particularly) were

just as bad, giving lead to the little children guiding them far, far from the things taught by that Prince.

While the Prince has been elevated to the unassailable position of deification, the ideas that he tried to get across didn't seem to make much of a dent, never mind a hole to let in a little fresh air, sunshine, and light.

One can almost picture Him sitting, chin in his right hand, with the left holding the arm near the elbow, and looking very sad. He gave but one commandment, and that is carefully ignored.

As we said in the first Cogitate of this series, modern plumbing hasn't helped a thing; at least before its advent, people had time to listen to and for that "still small voice" that guided one to the kingdom within.

It really doesn't take much cogitatin' to figure that if He was so important, then what he had to say was important, too — more important than the rush and hurry and the hypocritical and empty celebration of His birth.

Someday maybe we'll be able to build a society with the time to cogitate on that phrase: "I give ye but one commandment, that ye love one another", and the enemy to be overcome and conquered will be the enemy within.

Healing Today

Our continued thanks to Mr. Harry Edwards and Editor F. Terry Newman for permission to use material from THE SPIRITUAL HEALER (Published monthly by "The Healer Publishing Company Limited, Burrows Lea, Shere, Guildford, Surrey, England; yearly subscription $3.50 per year), and to Editor Mr. Maurice Barbanell for permission to use material from TWO WORLDS (Published monthly at 23 Great Queen Street, Kingsway, London, W.C.2, England; yearly subscription $2.80. Combined with a subscription to the weekly PSYCHIC NEWS, the fee of $10.50 represents a fair saving over separate subscriptions.)

EVERY ISSUE of *TWO WORLDS* contains material from the Spirit Guide, Silver Birch, under the general heading *Wisdom from the World Beyond*, while the specific collation will have its own title. In the July 1966 issue, the title was *There Are No Short Cuts to Spiritual Mastery*, and Silver Birch repeats here what he said to Harry Edwards some time ago, when Edwards visited the circle. The following paragraphs are reprinted by permission.

"I said something to him that he has used many times and I am very glad that he has done so. I said it is good to heal bodies and minds, but unless the soul come into its own the healing has failed. You have to touch souls.

"The sick man is at a spiritual crisis when he comes to you. It is then he has to make the turning point. Now he has a chance to begin to live as was intended. The sickness is a means of bringing him to spiritual understanding.

"If you heal the body and his spirit does not begin to express itself, then you have not succeeded, though it is not your fault. But if you can touch the soul, if you can allow the spirit to come into its own, then you are doing something no doctor, no clergyman, no scientist, no philosopher can possibly do.

"You are enabling the seeds of divinity to begin to express itself. As it does so, its association with the power that gave it birth begins to manifest and that soul begins to fulfill itself. Do not be disheartened if you cannot help all who come to you. The fact that they have come is their opportunity. You can only strive to serve."

HEALING SPIRITS

by Horace Leaf

THE BELIEF that invisible intelligences can help mankind seems to be as old as the human race. If modern primitive races are examples of their forebears the belief is justified. All modern so-called "primitive" races have a firm conviction that unseen spiritual forces are willing and able to come to the assistance of mankind, if approached in the proper manner, and one of their special favors is to cure diseases.

Years ago I witnessed the way Maoris invoked the aid of one of these spiritual forces. The scene was in commemoration or a great Maori warrior whose chief achievement appears to have been a clever ruse by means of which he had been able to exterminate a tribe with which he was at war; but he had other events to his credit.

His success is evidently still ascribed to the powerful *atua* or spirit who had guided his steps. Among other characteristics, this great chieftain had a most powerful *mana* of his own, by means of which good luck and good health could be assured, so long as his followers obeyed his wishes, which were fortified by the assistance of his mysterious *atua*. Hongi could both destroy and save, kill or cure by virtue of this spiritual force, influence or spirit.

This belief in the ability of spiritual powers to react on mankind is by no means extinct among civilized people, including many who will be historically great. Less than two generations ago the most famous psychiatrist, Cesare Lombroso, confessed his belief in spiritual aid, and admitted that he did not hestitate to seek help from this source whenever he felt it necessary. This is equally true of some of the ancient philosophers, including Socrates, whose "familiar" played such a large part in his affairs that skeptical historians are still unable to make up their minds what to do about it.

Quite a number of these spiritual influences have been named and play a conspicuous part in the faith of mankind today. Most of these forces played a leading part in religion and philosophy. A case in point is Gabriel the "messenger of God," mentioned not only in the Old and New Testaments, but also in the Koran, the scripture of Islam, the religion founded by Mahomet. Gabriel played a similar part as the messenger of God in the life of the mother of John the Baptist and Mary, the mother of Jesus. Spiritual influence, therefore, also played a part in the founding of Christianity.

Perhaps the most important spiritual force in this respect was Jahwey, the spirit so devoted to the Jewish race, and who from time to time, throughout the ages, manifested through the principal Hebrew Prophets. He appears to have made the question of health one of his chief interests, and produced amazing "miraculous" cures for ages, accounts of which are to be found in the Old and the New Testaments. Those whom he most influenced rank among the greatest of the world's spiritual healers.

It is notable that these spiritual beings leaned heavily towards religion, and regarded religion as playing a significant part in both the cure and infliction of disease.

That similar claims should still be made is not surprising. Spiritual healers evidently obtain their power from somewhere, and they should be the best judges of where it comes from especially since psychologists have been so assiduously plumbing the depth of the human mind.

Their plumbline has by no means reached the depth of human possibilities, but there remains much that appears to be explicable only by some kind of outside help. Unfortunately, many spiritual healers are ignorant of certain psychological associations, and unhesitatingly place the credit on some idea favored by tradition, even though it may not concur with modern research about the nature of the human mind.

THIS ATTITUDE usually causes the healer to attribute his cures to the direct interposition of God, forgetful of the laws through which He works. All monarchs are obliged to work through agents specially qualified for the particular duties they are to perform. The main law through which Nature works for the curing of mankind of diseases has always been medical men.

Raising the concept to the religious stage, the agents may take a more appropriate form. Mahomet realized this, and it has become a firm belief of his followers, many of whom are consummate spiritual healers, that God has delegated spiritual healing to specially qualified intelligences. According to Moslems, "Allah's sovereign will" can never be altered, and in that will is included the notion that cures can be wrought through His agents, spiritual as well as human.

The last few decades have seen enter the spiritual healing field large number of people who, through the revelations of psychic science, have come to believe that positive conditions can be induced which leave no room for doubt about the cooperation of healing spirits. This is no new discovery. The Ancient Greeks, Egyptians, Babylonians, Romans and others have left records showing why they believed similarly.

In the Bible plenty of evidence can be found, fully justifying the belief. Ezekiel records more than one personal experience of this actually taking place. In support he quotes instances: "The spirit entered into me when he spake unto me and set me upon my feet, that I heard him that spake unto me."

MANY YEARS AGO, when quite a neophyte in spiritual healing, I had the good fortune to be able to watch the development of this kind of spiritual healer from its inception. A fellow-student of mine who, like myself, aimed at devoting his whole life to religion as a Christian minister, became obsessed with the idea of quickly performing spiritual work among people. He therefore began to pray for the "gift of healing". I do not think he had a very clear idea of what form this could take so, like Micawber, he prayed and "waited for something to turn up".

For some time nothing unusual happened, and the prayer seemed in vain. Lookers-on regarded this aspiration as nothing more than an enthusiastic but nevertheless crazy idea of a cranky religionist; but, undeterred, his invocations continued to pour out. Then one Sunday evening, while sitting with a group on the lawn of our schoolmaster, chatting after church service, the company were astonished to see dropping from the young man's fingers phosphorescent globules. On drawing the young man's attention to this, he sprang up in alarm, vigorously shaking his hands, only to see a cloud of there globules fly through the air.

Shortly after this, groups were formed to encourage this strange phenomenon during which the young man passed into a trance from which he would awake totally unaware of what had transpired.

During these trances his personality would change, and he assumed in an unmistakable way the actions of an elderly man, who proceeded to work wonders with the mysterious power. I have seen him standing in the middle of the enthralled circle of people, kneading rapidly with his hands, after he had gone to one or other of the company, and made what can best be described as drawing passes from the back of the individual's head to the bridge of his nose. My father seemed to be the favorite subject for this.

From what appeared to be merely smoke, the kneading would cause to form a large round object about the size of a football,* from which would be emitted clouds of vapor which ascended towards the ceiling, but never reached before disappearing. By now the ball of phosphorescence would become semi-solid, and occasionally he would pitch it from him towards the wall. It would then disintegrate and disappear.

In the trance state he would speak in an unknown tongue, which in time developed into broken English. He then explained that he was the spirit of an ancient Zoroastrian priest who had come in answer to the young man's prayer to become a healer, and become a healer he did.

My parents opened their home for him to see his patients in, I being elected as master of ceremonies. I usually requested the patients to put on dark cloth-

ing, the better to see the healing power, for as he passed his hands over the patient everybody present could see the ten rays of light where his fingers passed. In view of this, it became impossible to deny the reality of healing magnetism, or, to use Mesmer's term, "animal magnetism", to distinguish it from magnetism of the magnet.

That the strange but wonderful spiritual influence that controlled my friend was most appropriate in its claim is obvious. Zoroastrians regard the Sun as the principal symbol of Creative Energy and Mind, and fire is in some way sacred and related to it. Furthermore, the claim that it had come in answer to my friend's prayer to help mankind in some useful spiritual way was fully justified by the results, for we had clear evidence of phosphorescence being a curative essence.

Even Ezekiel's experiences are not more convincing, as justification of the belief (and claim) that spiritual beings can participate in curing sick humans when circumstances are favorable.

*"Football" in Britain is more like American soccer than anything else, so a British football would be round rather than oval, like the American football.

QUESTIONS TO MR. EDWARDS

WHEN A PERSON seeks absent healing from Harry Edwards, Mr. Edwards requests that the subject keep in touch with him by correspondence. Some of the letters received pose questions of general interest. *THE SPIRITUAL HEALER** prints some of these in each issue, in the *Readers' Forum* department. Here are a few.

DIMINISHING EPILEPSY

My son's attacks have greatly diminished since you commenced intercessions. Sometimes there is only one slight one every week. Can I expect these to go completely? — R.S.B.

The answer is yes. With the soothing away of the tension causes in the mind, you will find that the attacks will be less strong and at greater intervals. The healing is progressive until the trouble is overcome. You should always try to keep your boy free from depression, over-excitement or disappointments — to keep him tranquil and contented.

PERMANENCE OF CURE

Since I wrote you three weeks ago, my shoulder joint, which had been semi-locked for many years, has suddenly become free, and glory be, all the pain has gone, too. Is this likely to be permanent? — S.H.

There is no reason why it should not be. We cannot foresee the future, but with normal care and avoidance of chill and dampness, it should remain well. If there should be any sign of the return of the trouble write us at once.

GOD'S HEALING

It is being repeatedly said that the work of doctors and surgeons is God's healing and is similar to spiritual healing. I cannot see this. Medical treatment is surely purely physical, whereas spiritual healing comes from a divine source. What are your views? — H.F.D.

In the practical sense we agree that while the two forms of healing can be comple-

---

*Mr. Leaf's article, appeared in the July 1965 issue, as did the questions and answers; the Testimonies of Healing come from the December 1965, all three items being reprinted by permission of the editor and Mr. Edwards.

mentary, they are separate processes within the universal laws. Yet though the surgeon sets the broken limb he does not *heal* it, though rendering it physically amenable to restoration. Fundamentally, all *healing* is divine.

* * *

VERSES THAT HELP

The enclosed two verses were given to my mother more than fifty years ago, when she was in great sorrow. They were of great comfort to her, and when I have been sad or very worried I have repeated them silently when I have gone to bed. They helped enormously. — M C.

Fearest thou the way before thee
Seemeth it to thee,
That the pathway all untrodden
Dark and rough must be?

Shrink not from the dread tomorrow,

Take thy rest tonight;
God may show a brighter pathway
In the morning light.

* * *

PSYCHOLOGICAL MEDICINE

I value your healing beyond all words; it has done me so much good. But can you give me a good herbal medicine or tonic? While I know this may be psychological, I feel I need it. — S. W.

I understand how you feel your need. I advise you to contact a good herbalist, in person or through the post, or alternatively to see your doctor or chemist. It is common sense that strengthening medicines, malt, vitamin preparations, are good for us, and these assist the healing by giving to a patient the means to increase his vitality and bodily resistance to ills and weaknesses.

TESTIMONIES OF HEALING

"Testimony" is something which the materialistic and "scientific" minded investigator is likely to scoff at, since from the strict viewpoint of the "scientific method" a person's opinion does not constitute evidence. The patient will say, "I suffered from so and so, and then I went to this healer (or wrote to this healer) and look, now I'm well." The "scientific" investigator then says, "Hum!" (and perhaps adds "bug" under his breath). "How do we know that you really suffered from the ailment you think you did? How do we know that it wouldn't have responded to ordinary competent medical treatment? How do we know you've really recovered?"

Now, actually, these are perfectly reasonable questions, and no true Healer resents them so long as the person asking them is really willing to *look* at the answers. Undoubtedly there are many instances in which a satisfactory answer cannot be given, particularly in an instance of absent healing. If someone who has requested absent healing later reports improvement or cure, the Healer will give thanks to God (the Source of all healing) but he might not include this case under the "cures" effected through his ministry. After all the Healer does not always *know* the full particulars in a case like this.

But the Healer will have in his records cases which have been treated by professionals, according the approved medical standards, cases which have been given up as hopeless. The honest doctor knows far too well from experience that there are many instances where everything he (and his colleagues) can do fail. Many cases of this sort have been either greatly improved (and note, this was a case where medical opinion stated that *no* improvement could be expected) or entirely cured. *Now* we have evidence.

Many doctors like to evade the issue by the use of such a term as "spontaneous remission" — which actually *explains nothing at all.* At the very best it describes something: it says in effect: "The patient did *not* respond to medicine, surgery, first aid, etc. — then suddenly recovered. It just happened, all by itself." And the argument that medical men want us to accept is that since it *did* happen, then it would have happened anyway, whether the patient had turned to Spiritual Healing or not. And the doctor speaking may cite some cases he knows of where this did happen without any recourse to Spiritual Healers. Let's assume he's honest; and since he is, he'll admit it's baffling, but suspects that there is some connection with the mind, psychosomatics (another word which describes but does not really explain), or whatever.

So the conventional doctor's response may be, "Well, yes, I cannot deny that we had this chain of events: a seemingly hopeless pathological condition, an appeal to Spiritual Healing, and a recovery. But scientifically speaking this just doesn't prove that Spiritual Healing works. We know that *something* happened—this blind man now sees, this deaf man now hears, this lame man now walks—but there is no proof that it was Spiritual Healing that made the difference. What about the case of X where the same thing happened without Spiritual Healing?"

A coincidence.

Well, yes, when it happens once or twice "coincidence" (another word which really doesn't explain anything) sounds reasonable enough.

But when "coincidences" take place day after day, week after week, year after year at the Healing Sanctuaries? Isn't it about time to report the matter to the Society for the Prevention of Cruelty to Coincidence? Coincidence is being loaded down with a greater burden than any word can bear!

We know (the Healers constantly state) that Spiritual Healing does not result in complete cures in 100% of the cases where it is sought. It does not result in notable or permanent improvement in 100% of the cases where it is sought, either. But the percentage where cure or improvement *has* occurred, and *continues to occur* is high enough to encourage people whose illnesses have not responded to conventional medical procedures to turn to the Healers.

Yes—perhaps *some* of these cases would have come under the doctor's handy "spontaneous remission" pigeon-hole; but to brush them all away thus cannot be considered as other than superstition—and, in his own way, no one can be as superstitious as the die-hard materialist.

Here, then, are some testimonies; the SPIRITUAL HEALER publishes only *very few* out of the thousands received by *one Healer;* we can only offer you a very few out of those that the *SPIRITUAL HEALER* publishes.

As someone noted, "Appearances are not deceiving if there are enough of them."

"I do hope you will not think I am troubling you with a trivial matter, but as you cured my mother of colitis I feel you would be able to help me. When my mother first wrote to you she was very ill, and the specialist at the hospital and her own doctor told her there was no cure for colitis and she would always have to exist on a very limited diet. However, thanks to you, her colitis has gone and she can now eat anything." — 60/136.

* * *

"You helped so much in your intercession for the young Catholic priest last year. I wrote to you several times telling you of the improvement, and after an absence of some months I have just hear that this has been maintained. We all send you our most grateful thanks." — 60/141.

* * *

"I am writing to ask if you will be good enough to seek healing for me again. Some years ago I was suffering from hernia, and you made intercession, with the result that although I still wear a very light truss, the hernia is to all intents and purposes completely cured. I have traveled across America,

THE CONTEMPLATIVE LIFE

by Joel S. Goldsmith

A New Text for Personal Growth and Extended Awareness

THE CONTEMPLATIVE LIFE is a guide-book to attainment of inner peace and joy for those who are seeking a way to live a full and complete life here and now. Joel Goldsmith explains how to bridge the gap between the distractions of the outer world and the silence of the inner world through God-contact.

How the mind can transcend its apparent limitations and become what it is intended to be, an instrument for the free flowing of the Spirit, is specifically explained by the author in his description of the resources available in meditation.

Goldsmith, author of *The Infinite Way* and *The Thunder of Silence*, in his latest volume brings fresh insight to the practice of contemplation and meditation in everyday living.

THE CONTEMPLATIVE LIFE

is priced at $4.50

ORDER FROM PAGE 130

swam, played tennis — and there has been no recurrence of the trouble. It is a sheer miracle."
—60/154.

*   *   *

"My wife had disseminated sclerosis, and Mr. Edwards commenced absent healing at my request — much to the disgust of my wife, who was hostile to the whole thing. During the following three months my wife made a marvellous recovery. The help was real, particularly at night, when the nerves 'twisted' and 'screwed.' This was particularly noticeable in the limbs. Gradually, too, the bowels and bladder improved. I came to the obvious conclusion that applied help was coming from somewhere, and so did my wife. Her right leg was very poor, and the doctor suggested a calliper, which was refused and, in fact,

was never required. My wife's health was never better than at the moment, and we had the arrival of a son on Sunday last."
—40/177.

*   *   *

"I must tell you the good news. A dear friend was brushing up her hearth a year ago when she toppled over and one hand went into the red-hot fire. It was burnt horribly. You had her on your prayer list. Yesterday she told me her doctor said her recovery was a perfect miracle, he cannot understand it. The wound healed so quickly and has not even left a scar, and usually a bad burn of that nature draws up all the muscles and closes the fingers. Her hand is perfectly normal. My friend is interested in your work, and attributes her recovery to spiritual healing." — 60/200.

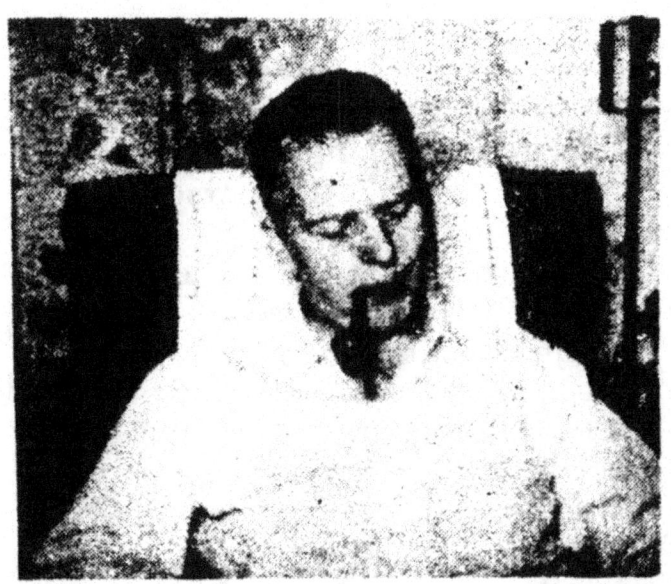

Love vs. love

"'LOVE' AS IT is commonly thought of is a two-way proposition. In other words, you can't really love someone unless they love back. I think that most anyone will agree with me on this point." (1)

I **agree** that love *is* very commonly thought of this way, and this implies a definition of love. I do not agree that this definition has anything to do with the "Love" that the great philosophers and the great religious teachers speak of; or the tireless evolved Spirits who continue their job of living in other parts of the One universe and select as part of their job communi-

cating and guiding those of us in this part of the One universe who are willing to listen.

No one can exhaust the glossary of what Love "is", and words and the limitations of words can be reached long before more than a fraction of a definition can be reached. And you might think that this is a rather peculiar subject for discussion in a magazine entitled *EXPLORING THE UN-KNOWN*—not that "Love" doesn't involve a great deal of unknown-ness, but isn't that a better subject for *REAL LIFE GUIDE TO SEX AND MAR-RIAGE,* or a psychology magazine? Well, of course, it's a good subject for both, but it belongs here, too. It belongs both in what you might loosely call the scientific and the religious aspects of this publication, since we are concerned not only with what psychic phenomena *are,* but what they are *for*—that involves living beings, mostly human beings; relationships; and Love is a measuring stick in this frame of reference.

I am going to use a typographical gimmick in order to differentiate between the sort of love that is being talked about; lower case "love" denotes the sort that is described in the quotation with which we started; upper case "Love" denotes the genuine article.

You can love *EXPLORING THE UNKNOWN,* meaning that you are very fond of the publication, you look forward to each issue; you felt a sense of loss when (as has happened, alas, too often in the past) you had to wait an extra month for the next issue; you felt a certain affection towards various of the contributors whose writings you responded to with pleasure.

But you could not possibly Love *EXPLORING THE UNKNOWN.*

You can only Love a person. You do not have to know the person or even like the person:

you can still wish the best for this person; you can be willing to do something for this person which you feel this person needs and you are able to do; and you can do this whether or not the person reciprocates to an equal degree, or reciprocates at all, for that matter. You can take personal risks for what you believe to be this person's welfare, and you can do this even if the particular person hates you and actively seeks your damage or destruction as we think of destruction in this part of the universe.

You *can* do it; it is possible. Which does not mean that you will do it, necessarily.

And the same applies as a possibility in regard to every other human being, in relation to yourself, on this planet, because Love is an expression of one's being, and not a contract — not something which is absolutely dependent upon someone else's reciprocation. It cannot ever be perfect in this stage of our life, because there just aren't any perfect people. When we think of perfection in relation to Love, we can only think of God, first. But this doesn't help very much; better to think of God's manifestations through human beings who demonstrated Love — or who demonstrate — they aren't all gone from our immediate ken.

ARE THERE any over-all definitions? Yes, there are some that are sufficient; I think that the finest short one can be found in a widely-reprinted letter. (2)

The letter-writer starts out by saying that if you do not have Love, then nothing you do and nothing you become — in the sense of success in this present part of your life — is going to be of any real or lasting good for *you*. You can be a great leader or teacher — political, scientific, military, religious, etc. — the Greatest; but if you do not have Love in your being, then you'll still be a Nothing within yourself, and no amount of outer success will give you the inner realization of being a person.

You can have the sort of psychic powers which make it possible for you to do things which people will call miraculous; you can study and learn all manner of ESP techniques and demonstrate them to an awesome degree — but without Love in you, it all becomes dust and ashes. Without Love, none of this will satisfy *your* inner being, whatever it may do for other people. You can win the world's record for Good Works, even wind up as the greatest of martyrs, for the greatest of causes — but without Love, all that adds up to exactly nothing, so far as you are concerned,

and does not make you anything at all.

Why? Is it possible to do tremendous things without Love?

Yes, it is. Think for a moment of Adolf Hitler. He was a Great Leader; no one can deny that. He offered hope to millions of people who were in despair. They listened to him; they lifted up their heads, and began to rebuild shattered lives.

He did not have Love in him. He wanted to rebuild a wrecked and ruined nation because he hated; he wanted to make a diminished nation world-feared because he hated. Yet, despite the fact that he preached hatred and practised violence, he brought hope to millions, who thought he was a messiah, a saviour. We tend to forget that there must have been those in Germany who were truly inspired to good by this greatest of contemporary haters, and who were not corrupted by him.

But we also know that Hitler was Nothing inside himself — nothing but a great resentment, a screaming hate, a vessel of wrath that finally destroyed itself. Yet (and this is important) there were those close to him who, even after the terrible end, thought him a good and kindly man, driven by wicked enemies to harsh measures at times.

The point is, that even if Hitler had not gone the full path of destruction — even if he had been stopped while millions still blessed him — he would still have been Nothing, so far as his own welfare was concerned.

A lesser and more common example is the so-called "do-gooder" who may actually do a lot of good things, but is motivated by other considerations than Love; many notable heroes and martyrs have been informed by envy, self-seeking, etc.

THE WRITER of the letter referred to above offers what amounts to a series of tests. Only a perfect human being would be able to pass them all, but if a person cannot pass any of them, we can be pretty sure that Love doesn't live here. I'm going to quote a few excerpts.

"This love of which I speak is slow to lose patience — it looks for a way of being constructive."

Lover-case love is generally quite the opposite; it becomes very impatient when frustrated or not reciprocated. It worries about whether the object is "worthy". It may conceal impatience for a time, but underneath the mask is the constant demand for its own due and rights. It may go through constructive periods (when everything is as it desires), but when the stopping point is reached, it does not look for ways of being constructive.

It is not possessive; it is neither anxious to impress nor does it cherish inflated ideas of its own importance."

Lower-case love is a contract sort of thing. It makes demands and insists upon its own rights and dues. It asserts "self", but this sort of self is a very childish one; it is parasitical. It wants exclusive possession, wants to absorb and envelop, where Love seeks no more than an opportunity to share — without making demands.

A well-known psychotherapist (3) has this observation to make upon that alleged great lover, Romeo. " . . . Romeo, in displaying his ardent romantic passion for Juliet, also showed how unloving he really was. For instead of saying to himself, when he thought that Juliet was dead, 'What a pity it is that this poor girl has gone! But I'm still alive. Now why don't I go out into the wide, wide world again and find someone *else* to love?' he obviously said to himself: 'Now that poor Juliet's kicked the bucket, and obviously no longer loves *me*, I am once again reduced to being the worthless slob I was before she came along to make me worthy of living, so I might as well end my pitiful existence.' Which he forthrightly did."

In the same chapter, the author describes Shakespeare's Antony as " . . . a kook who loved himself so little that he just couldn't bear to face life without Cleo's helping breast — not to mention without Caesar's and Rome's plaudits. This may seem, on the face of it, like death-less devotion to Cleopatra. But looked at a little more closely, it is really a lifeless lack of devotion to himself — to Antony."

For Love, of course, has to start with oneself. Lower-case love has to be possessive, because it springs from lack of any genuine self-love and is trying futilely to fill an empty void that cannot be filled that way. If one Loves oneself, one is not impatient with one's own faults, but seeks to be constructive — which does not mean saying, "Well, that's the way I am", and drifting along. Upper-case Love does not make unrealistic or absolute demands either of itself or anyone else. Lower-case love does just this; fails, of course; so *must* (it feels) possess the love and admiration of others in order to feel worthy of living at all.

But others to which it turns are in the same boat; all are empty or at best partly filled vessels, which cannot run over. So what we have is a contract:

"You love me as I want to be loved, and I'll love you after my fashion;

"You over-look my faults, and I'll over-look yours so long as they don't annoy me too much;

"You indulge my vices and I'll indulge yours, so long as you don't ask too much;

"You be true to me, and I'll be true to you, so long as nothing else comes along that's too good to resist, etc."

Both parties are constantly on the lookout for violations, and both feel that the other hasn't fulfilled his or her share of it.

Upper-case Love desires the best for the person loved, starting with oneself, but does not define that "best" in a strictly material sense. It does not demand. It may exhort, but if it does so, it exhorts in a way which does not violate others' rights to pay no attention if they are not interested. Lower-case love demands and nags constantly; it just knows that it's own opinions are *right*, and no one has the right to go against them. Upper-case Love simply is not concerned about how wonderful its opinions are and is not positive that everyone should agree with them.

"Love has good manners

*and does not pursue selfish ad-
vantage. It is not touchy. It does
not keep account of evil or gloat
over the wickedness of other
people. On the contrary, it is
glad with all good men when
truth prevails.*

Lower-case love may be very
much concerned with etiquette,
the counterfeit of good manners,
and does not hesitate to exploit
its object in order to gain what
it considers as advantages. "For
your own good" is often its slo-
gan, and while this may be conscious hypocrisy at times it is
more often self-deception. The
person who has Love may, indeed, have social, political, national, etc., preferences — but is
not delighted to hear scandal
about *them* which can be turned
to *our* advantage, nor does it
feel bad when *they* show up
somewhat better than *us* at times.

*"Love knows no limit to its
endurance, no end to its trust,
no fading of its hope; it can
outlast anything. It is, in fact,
the one thing that still stands
when all else is fallen.*

Now some will read this and
think that the author of this
quotation is preaching pure
masochism, saying that if you
just can't "take" everything
without complaint, then you
don't Love — and nuts to that.
I'll say "amen" to what they
think they are talking about,

but what they think they are
talking about and what our
author has said are quite different things.

First of all, Love does not
go out looking for opportunities
to suffer, even though a lot of
people who *are* looking for opportunities to suffer, *say* that
they are doing it out of Love.
They aren't, whatever they may
have convinced themselves.
Love does not seek self-damage,
but it does accept risks, does
accept the possibility of suffering
right up to and including un-
pleasant manners of decease.
People who die for something
they say they Love (particularly
if there is some sort of religious
connotation) are called martyrs.
Many such people were not martyrs; many of them were fools
or in a state of serious emotional
disturbance — but the counterfeit
does not impeach the genuine
object. There have been genuine
martyrs, but none of them went
looking for martyrdom. Very
likely they prayed (as did Jesus
the Christ) that the "cup" might
be put aside from them; genuine
Love in them enabled them to
continue to take the risk which
finally became an actuality. (4)

The thing is: Love does not
set limits to what it will endure,
while lower-case love considers
that really, one has to draw the
line somewhere. Since none of
us are perfect, even one who

Loves may decide at a certain point, "no farther", but this is not something settled in advance. Lower case love is terribly worried about its splendors being wasted; upper case Love knows inwardly that Love cannot be wasted, and isn't worried about the question. Lower-case love stays pretty much on the same level, except when it deteriorates; while with Love—its capacities increase with Loving.

And what about that well-known phrase, "loving the unlovable"? The "unlovable" referred to is not someone whom you dislike, or whom no one likes, etc; the "unlovable" is a person who refuses to accept Love, who responds to Love with hate. Obviously an impossible case for the person who believes that you just can't love someone if someone doesn't love back. But not for one who has Love.

And in the end, Love is realistic; lower-case love is not so at all. RAWL

NOTES

(1) Creath Thorne, in the letter section of *WARHOON* #21; the present editorial is drawn from the reply the I made in *WARHOON* #22. (The publication was an amateur one with a very limited circulation, and has since been discontinued due to the press of other commitments and interests on the part of the publisher.)

(2) Paul's first letter to the Corinthians, chapter thirteen; the quotations are from the paraphrase of the New Testament made by J. B. Philips.

(3) Albert Ellis, Ph.D. The quotations are from the chapter, "Sick and Healthy Love", in his book, *If This Be Sexual Heresy*. Some of the Dr. Ellis's notions of "healthy" love may be open to question, but I think he describes what he considers "sick" love very well.

(4) In *Murder in the Cathedral,* Thomas a'Becket is visited by four tempters, the fourth of which urges him to seek martyrdom as the only solution to his dilemma. Thomas replies in a soliloquoy that " . . . the last temptation is the greatest treason/to do the right deed for the wrong reason." He does accept martyrdom, rather than make the compromises that would, so far as he knows, spare his life; but he does not try to get himself killed.

For many years I have thought of Giordano Bruno as the sort of self-damaging masochist who finally managed to get himself killed unpleasantly by his enemies, so that he could wind up as a "martyr". Now I am not so sure; after all, the temper of this age is to present almost anyone who is "martyred" for reasons that might be considered religious as very neurotic and subconsciously dedicated to self-destruction.

Odd Facts Of Science

by JERRYL L. KEANE, Ph.D.

(author of How Valid Is Psychic Phenomena? Psychism vs. Mediumship, etc.)

IF ONE PROWLS around in the dustier corners of any good-sized library, uncovering odd and little known facts about scientific discoveries, inventions, and theories down through the ages can be both a rewarding and an enlightening pastime.

For the most part, the dates given in text and history books refer only to the earliest date that several people of considerable importance began to notice something that had been known, but unrecognized for many centuries. Many of the things that we know as common today, and consider "recently" discovered, invented, or formulated, can be traced back for many centuries; and the actual origins are lost in the dim mists of time.

Here are a few examples of such cases.

About the year 100 *A.D.*, a mathematician named Hero lived in the city of Alexandria in Egypt. He was a famous man, even in his own day, for not only did he solve several mathematical problems vital to our present day mathematics, but he was an inventor as well. These inventions included a double forcing pump suitable for a fire engine, and — hold your breath — a workable steam engine. Now according to our history books, the steam engine was invented by one James Watt of Scotland, seventeen hundred years later! This is not to belittle Mr. Watt's contribution to our society in the least; but just imagine what this world would be like if, in the first century, more people had paid attention to Hero's work and it had been taken up and followed through. Practically every "modern innovation", potentially at least, could have come about at least fifteen hundred years earlier.*

Just as interesting to us today are the satellites of Mars. According to the history books, these bodies were "discovered" and "first observed" in 1877 . . . but were they? Jonathan Swift, of *Gulliver's Travels* fame, observed in some of his writings, that the planet Mars had two "moons" and that the inner one, toward the planet, was swinging around Mars faster than Mars was turning on its orbit.

This has always been considered a "lucky guess" because at the time that Swift wrote it (according to present-day historians), the telescope had only been invented in 1608 by a Flemish optician named Lippershey.

Swift lived from 1677 to 1745. According to the historians, it is unlikely that Swift even knew what a telescope was, except possibly by hearsay. However, one of his own countrymen, three centuries earlier, had very clearly written out the instructions for making a telescope which would "make the stars appear as near as we please". This man's name was Roger Bacon; and seeing that he was also an extremely famous man, it is unlikely that his work was completely ignored.

It is also unlikely that Mars' moons had not been discovered in Swift's day. Much that was done during the period either was not recorded, or the records have been lost.

According to the known principles of physics, a natural body cannot orbit around its parent body faster than the

*Hero's steam engine was not ignored by the intelligent rulers of the day. Both Greek and Roman society was based upon slave labor, and the conclusions were that such advantages that might come from the use of steam engines would hardly be worth the price of a shattered economic system, as well as insurrection. Some of those who decided to bury Hero's steam engine, of course, were concerned with their own political and economic power and position; but some honestly believed that the cost in misery would be greater than the gains was worth. It would be well to study the lot of the common people during the Industrial Revolution, which took place in societies based on "free" labor before passing judgment on earlier societies. RAWL

parent body itself is turning, so for nearly one hundred years it was easier to ignore the idea. of such a thing happening, than it was to give somebody in history credit for it. However, today the scientists are beginning to realize that this "moon" must be an artificial satellite, which could act in such a manner, as the satellites which we have put into orbit prove.

For centuries most people have taken it for granted that "life" did not and could not exist anywhere in the universe except on our small ball of mud. Gradually it is dawning on everybody that we are very, very wrong.

Of course, too, until quite recently, "everybody knew" that what was solid was solid, and atoms were solid. Still, it would seem that a few people knew centuries before the atom got "split" that matter was an appearance and not a fact.

There was, for instance, Ruggiero Boscovich, a Jesuit astronomer and optician. Around the middle of the 18th century he wrote that "atoms were nothing but the centers of forces or powers" . . . and this man was not, in his own day, considered a metaphysical crackpot by his fellow scientists. In fact, he was of sufficient importance for the Royal Society to elect him as a Fellow. Even today, this is no small honor. Michael Faraday, the noted electrician of a century later, was well acquainted with and quoted Boscovich's work.

During the last half of the last century, when electricity began to be brought under control, many, many men began to investigate it and to invent machines operated by this then new, and still mysterious, power. Anything which was not almost immediately commercially adaptable fell by the wayside and was lost. Yet many of the ideas expressed in the reports to societies, and in books published at the time, which have been ignored by scientists and laymen alike, contain a mine of potential for development.

One of the lesser known inventions — never, unfortunately, completed — was very much on Thomas Alva Edison's mind until the day of his death.

Edison, like so many other truly great scientists, such as Burbank, William James, Sir William Crookes, Sir Oliver Lodge, Dr. Raynor C. Johnson, and a host of others, was convinced that conscious life was not dependent upon a physical body, but continuous through eternity. He was also convinced, as the others were, by evidence that he had received, that communication between the incarnate and discarnate states was occurring constantly through what are known as "mediums" or "psychic sensitives", and that a machine could be built which would enable anybody who operated it to communicate with those who were no longer in physical bodies. Edison himself left his physical body before the work on the instrument could be completed.

Was Edison wrong? Well, Edison invented the electric light, the gramophone, motion pictures, and a good many other things. In all, he took out over 1,000 patents on his inventions; and a sufficient number of these inventions are still in use so that we should pause to think before we discredit his intelligence (or the intelligence of other men of great scientific stature who agreed with this).

Many people from every walk of life and every society are convinced that this is true. "Orthodox" science, for the most part, turns up its collective nose and attempts to ignore the evidence. But are these scientists, and ourselves, right in taking such an attitude? The evidence is strong; it is strong enough so that many Universities have established investigation teams. Surely, scientifically speaking, those scientists who have been and are investigating such evidence are not spending years of research on something that does not exist.

More likely this is one of the places where the evidence which has been insisted on by so many sources has been consistently ignored and sneered at by the people who should have had at least enough curiosity to check.

This looks very much like another "Odd Fact of Science" that has been overlooked too long.

BOOKS

We receive far more books dealing with psychic phenomena, spiritual healing, development, and other subjects referring to the world of the unknown than it is possible for us to cover in this department. The listing of a book under the "Books Received" section does not impy that we consider these books poor, bad, or unworthy of consideration, but rather it seemed to us that the books you see reviewed were the **most** relevant to our readers. Wherever possible, the address of the publisher is given; in any event, books listed here should be ordered from the publishers, not from EXPLORING THE UNKNOWN. If you make such orders, we should, of course, greatly appreciate your mentioning that you saw the review here. The Editor takes full responsibility for reviews signed RAWL; all other reviewers are given as wide latitude as possible, but the views expressed by them do not necessarily coincide with those of the Editor (Why should they?)

THE GIFT OF HEALING

by Ambrose A. Worrall, with
Olga N. Worrall

Harper and Row, New York, 1965, $3.95, 220pp.

The Worralls are two of the very few genuine Spiritual healers we have in this country, and this book has been written by them in an effort to tell people about Spiritual Healing as they see it and have experienced it. The book is a sound one, devoid of cheap sensationalism, and packed with incidents which have occurred to them.

Both of these people have been unusually aware of their psychic gifts since childhood, and both consider these gifts something to be used — not flaunted — for the benefit of others, and to prove not only the continuity of life and communication between the various stages, but to heal others whenever and wherever it is possible for them to channel healing through. Mrs.

Worrall heads up the healing clinic at the Mt. Washington Methodist Church in Baltimore, and many of the cases which have resulted in healing through the services of the Worralls in this clinic are discussed.

Mr. Worrall has also told at some length about the psychic development of them both — how he healed his wife on occasion, how his and her, clairvoyance and clairaudience have enabled them to not only help others, but to guide themselves through their lives so that they could achieve a more meaningful existence.

As Mr. Worrall makes it very clear in the book, we are all psychics; and the slow development of our spiritual awareness, not gimmicks and gadgets, is what is needed in order to bring to the fore the gifts which are latent in all of us.

Adequate and responsible testimony to the facts which Mr. Worrall presents throughout the book is given for the accuracy of their clairvoyance and healing. Doctors have investigated and agreed that *something* has happened which is medically unexplainable when cures (of medically "incurable" people) have stemmed from the treatment which they have received from the Worralls.

Mr. Worrall also discusses the methods which he and his wife have developed and use in their healing activities, and urges others to develop their own gifts.

Probably the most amazing part of this book, for an American publication, is its lack of sensationalism. The Worralls are genuine, and, like this reviewer, feel that the truth is sufficiently sensational without trimmings, and that it is only by working with it in a sane, sensible way, that it can be of any real value in life.

This book is an absolute "must" for anyone who is truly interested in gaining a greater understanding of what we can call "God's purpose" in existence. Like all true workers in this field, they do not seek to "convert" anyone from his own religious group; they are convinced that the theological doctrines are not able to place a fence around the manifestation. Their purpose is simply to help those who turn to them. They do have an "absent healing" list, and will "send" to those at a distance, just as the English healers do.

We cannot recommend this book too highly to those who are seeking anything from understanding to healing; and the reviewer's personal thanks must be extended to the Worralls for writing a sane, reasonable, and most helpful book which tells the truth simply and clearly and opens the windows for a little fresh air and sunshine amid the confusion of what is normally published in this area here.

NEW BOTTLE— NEW WINE
by William L. Klug

Parastudy, Inc., Valleybrook Road, Chester Heights, Penna., 1963, 28 pp., $1.00

MAN'S INNER HUNGER— MAN'S FULFILLMENT

Same author, same publisher, 12 pp., 1966, 50 cents

Here we have two very interesting little booklets exploring from the angle of our present scientific expression, the ideas of God, eternity, and the structure of the Universe.

This writer is concerned with the application of what we call "quantum mechanics" to the operation of the Spiritual forces of existence, and the comparisons which can be made between what little we know of the nature of the Universe of spiritual levels with respect to our physics on this level. He comes up with some ideas which require a good deal of consideration and much careful thought; for "quantum mechanics" can, as he points out, apply to spiritual operation and the spiritual equivalent to matter as much as it does to matter and field physics.

For those who are interested in the psychic and spiritual manifestations from this angle, these thought-provoking booklets are well worth careful and serious study, for the "breakthrough" in our understanding is very apt to be made from this angle of study.

A MODERN MYSTIC SPEAKS
by Joseph Busby

"Voice" publishers, 8 Watling Road, Southwick, Sussex, England, 1965, 200 pp., $4.00 (softbound)

Joseph Busby is editor of a newspaper dedicated to world brotherhood called *The Voice*. The volume of his works considered here is an anthology of his short writings.

Like most of the English writers in this field, Joseph Busby uses a practical approach to mysticism — an approach which does some badly needed re-evaluating and which helps to clear some of the confusion from our minds and thinking. He points to methods which he, and others, have found valuable for the development of a wider consciousness and a greater understanding.

This book will particularly appeal to those who seek a deeper meaning to their theological teachings, although it is apt to leave the scientifically minded person rather cold. However, a careful study of its pages, plus a bit of experiment with his suggestions, would help the scientifically minded person to gain a bit of insight on what the religiously minded person is talking about.

The difficulty with Mr. Busby's work lies not in what he is doing and writing, but in the inadequacy of the English language to convey the basic religious concepts to the untrained person. All writers in this field face this problem, and Mr. Busby is to be praised for the care he has taken to overcome it, insofar as he is able to, using the particular approach to the Universal truth which he has.

There is, however, plenty of this type of material in this country, mostly published under various groups more or less connected with the White Brotherhood (of which Mr. Busby seems to be one of the English outlets) so that we feel that the translation of the price of 21/-d (in reality $2.96 currently) to $4.00 is rather "soaking the American" unnecessarily.

In spite of that, for the person building a selective library on mysticism, this book is worth buying.

THE PSYCHIC FACULTIES AND THEIR DEVELOPMENT
by Helen Macgregor and Margaret V. Underhill

London Spiritualist Alliance (now College of Psychic Science) 16 Queensbury Place, London, SW 7, England, 76 pp, 1947, 60 cents postpaid. (Introduction by Robert Fielding Gould, MA, MD, MRCP.)

This is one of a series of booklets which the former LSA put out some years ago, which is still, fortunately, in print and available for one who wishes to develop communication with those who have gone beyond our normal sight, but not beyond reach of our senses and theirs — that is, not beyond if one is sincere and willing to attempt to develop the means of communication intelligently.

One of the truly great advantages of the English Spiritualist group is their insistence that this is for "everybody" and that everyone has abilities which can be developed simply, safely and sanely, in the same sense that "everyone" can learn to play a musical instrument or learn to draw a recognizable picture. True, there are few truly great musicians and/or painters in the world; and for the same reason there are few truly great mediums and communicators. But until the latent ability is tapped and trained, no ability whatsoever can be demonstrated, whether it be musicianship, painting or mediumship; and learning communication, like learning anything else, brings wider horizons and areas of activity into our lives. With the attempt to learn, comes the surfacing of abilities which we did not know we had. Hence, learning communication with friends and relatives whom we love, who have gone into another stage of existence, can and does give us the assurance that we are continuous through time and space, no matter how limited we may be in the present stage of existence. We can start here and now to push back those limitations and eventually succeed in accomplishing things which seem impossible on this level.

This book then gives a "rundown" on the various types of mediumship and practical ways in which to develop the various types; the material is based on years of experiment and testing. It contains as precise directions as possible for almost every type of mediumship known, including a short bit on psychic photography — something which does need a great deal more work and experimentation than it has had to date.

This is a good, practical book for those who wish to develop and explore in a reasonable manner, and the following through of the instructions given will result in the building of a firm link; it includes warnings of the pitfalls in "pushing" development ahead too far and too fast for the individual to take safely.

The majority of those interested in this type of development in this country of "Instant Everything" tend to approach this business with the idea that any gimmick or gadget which will speed up the process (such as hypnotism or the psychedelic drugs) is a good and reliable idea. Those who have such ideas should read this book merely for the information contained about over-rapid development by artificial means such as this. Like everything else, learning speed is bound to vary with the individual; but there is a difference between a person who is inherently conditioned, with the psychic faculties close to the surface and therefore rapid in development, and the one who uses artificial means which place psychic reception beyond control.

This, too, is a "must" in the library and reading for anyone interested in proving the continuity of life to himself by means of personal experience.

INVISIBLE HORIZONS

by Vincent Gaddis

Chilton Books, Philadelphia, 1965, 240 pp with index, $4.25.

For anyone who wants a really good piece of light reading about some of the mysteries which have arisen with sea travel, this is the book for them.

Mr. Gaddis, bless him, has the good sense to research his material well, present the facts very well, and, praises be, avoid the cheap sensationalism which usually accompanies this sort of writing.

Each of the fifteen stories contained in this book has its own biographical data in a section in the back of the book, just before the well-done index, so that the reader whose curiosity leads him to further investigation about any of the incidents listed has a handy reference for starting on his search. There is also a world map in the front of the book with an extended list of legends, so that the reader may pinpoint the area in which each incident written about occurred.

While it is true that most of this material has been published previously in one form or another, there is a difference between writing "wild tales", however basically true, and responsible reporting such as has been done by Mr. Gaddis in this volume. Far from the interest being lost by such treatment, it is brought forth with credibility that there are many things happening all the time all over our planet that cannot be "explained away".

We highly recommend this book, and wish that more writers in this field would show a similar sense of responsibility for writing the unvarnished truth about such happenings. We hope this author will do another equally creditable job of writing about "mysterious" happenings in the near future.

FROM MESMER TO CHRISTIAN SCIENCE

by Frank Podmore

It is really a shame that University Press feels obliged to place such a high price on the reprints of the famous classics which they are doing, for while they do a superb printing and binding job, their prices place badly-needed reference books out of the reach of the average person who is trying to build a small, sound library of this material.

This book, originally written during the first decade of this century, is a careful study of the healing movement in general, highlighting some of the most remembered leaders of it from Mesmer to M.B. E., plus many tests, incidents and researches which have been carefully buried under a lot of modern-day terminology and/or ignored.

Like all the early research, there was the faction which was looking at these effects and trying to understand them, and the faction which was avoiding looking at them and, if faced with them, explaining them away with a wave of the hand, or putting on a determined campaign to disprove them. During the Podmore period, there was one major difference and that was that *both* sides were published and heard; and it is this which makes this book, and

the other reports from that general period, so interesting, valuable, and informative.

Frank Podmore, among others, knew what he was talking about both from research and from first hand experience. The book is well researched and annotated, and, as it is closer to the period involved by over fifty years, closer to the truth; for the legends and embroideries had not had the time to garnish the underlying facts involved.

This is a "must on the shelf, and for the reading" by anyone who wants sane, sensible material in this field, without either the raving of the enthusiasts or the "poo-poohs" of those who refuse to consider.

We hope that University Press will be able to see their way in the very near future to put out soft cover editions, of these great classics at a nominal price, so that good literature in this field will have a wider distribution than is possible at their current prices and editions.

BOOKS RECEIVED

SHE FOLLOWS THE PSYCHIC PATH (Psychic Experiences of Jessie Shaver Jones), edited by Ruth Shaver; Vantage Press, New York, 1964, 48 pp. $2.00.

MY LORD IS THE TREE OF LIFE, by Billie Alonzo; copies free from author, P.O. Box 1571, Kansas City, Mo. 172 pp. Paperback.

THEY SPEAK WITH OTHER TONGUES, John L. Sherrill; a Pyramid Book, New York, 1964, 143 pp. (with references) 60¢ Paperback.

HEAL THYSELF by Edward Bach M.B., Bs., D.P.H.; C. W. Daniel Company Limited, Ashingdon, Rochford, Essex, England, 1962 (7th edition), 56pp. 70¢ (postpaid) Paperback.

JOURNEY INTO SPIRIT WORLD by Bertha Harris; the Spiritualist Association of Great Britain, 33 Belgrave Square, London, S.W.1. England, 37 pp. 70¢ (postpaid) Paperback.

WHAT ARE YOU? by Imelda Octavia Shanklin; Unity School Of Christianity, Lee's Summit, Mo., 1965 (11th edition) 160 pp. Paperback, no price listed.

VARIETIES OF MYSTIC EXPERIENCE by Elmer O'Brien; Mentor-Omega Books New York, 1964, 252 pp. (with bibliography and appendix) 75¢ Paperback.

THE BRONZE AGE GOD IN THE SPACE AGE by Cline Clark; Exposition Press, New York, 1965, 43 pp. $2.75.

EDGE OF TOMORROW by Henry Mangum, Ph.D., Vantage Press, New York, 1965, 174 pp. (with sources) $2.95.

THE WAY OF THE MYSTIC by Evan Teller; Exposition Press, New York, 1965, 194 pp. $5.00.

IT SHALL BE CONQUERED by Jo Leslee; Christopher Publishing House Boston, 1962, 181 pp. $3.75.

THE FLOWERING TREE by Gladys V. Jones; William Sloane Associates, New York, 1965, 316 pp. (with bibliography) $4.95.

LET'S PEEL AN ONION by Sonja Henry; Vantage Press, New York, 1965, 128 pp. (with appendix) $2.75.

SURPRISING MYSTICS by Herbert Thurston, S. J., (edited by J. H. Crehan, S. J.), Henry Regnery Company, Chicago, 1955, 138 pp. (with index) $6.50.

THE PARALYZING RAYS VS. THE NUCLEARS by Guido (Skipper) Nizzi; Vantage Press, New York, 1964, 185 pp. $3.00.

AUTOACTION, THE LAW OF ONE by Leith Robertson; Exposition Press, New York, 1965, 29 pp. (with epilogue) $3.00.

SPIRITUAL EVOLUTION, VIA CAUSE AND EFFECT by Richard Durant; Vantage Press, New York, 1965, 127 pp. $2.95.

THE INNER PATH TO GOD by Swami Premananda; Vantage Press, New York, 1964, 123 pp. $3.50.

YOU ARE THAT by Mabel B. Peck; Vantage Press, New York, 1965, 148 pp. $3.50.

SECRETS OF YOUR SUPRACONSCIOUS by Walter M. Germain; Hawthorn Books, Inc., Publishers, New York, 1965, 274 pp. (with bibliography) $5.95.

The Eyrie

All letters and other written communication from readers are welcome, and are considered for inclusion in this department, if we can read them at all, unless the writer specifically states that his communication (or a specified part of it) is not for publication. Letters must be signed and bear the writer's full address, if publication is desired; we will withhold the writer's name, or address, or both if this is requested. The editor reserves the right to abridge letters, but most of them are published complete.

WE REGRET that the length of Ursula Roberts' fine essay, *Hints on Mediumistic Development,* is such that we could not bring it all to you in one issue. However this is not fiction, and it does break quite naturally into three parts; you can read each installment as it appears or save up the three issues. It is not, of course, a complete course in mediumship; what Miss Roberts has set out to do—and we feel that she has done it very well, which is why we arranged to reprint this essay—is to give you a general idea of just what mediumship is (and by exclusion, what it

is not). We all have some sort of psychic talent (some of us more than one); this talent, or these talents, will lie "nearer the surface" in one person than another. In the broadest possible sense of the word, we *all* have the potentiality to be *mediums for the transmission of Divine Light to our fellow human beings.* However, the word "medium" is generally thought of as referring to a person through whom discarnates send communications to persons living here on Earth. The *value* of such messages varies widely, and can be broken down into two categories (a) evidence designed to satisfy a person or persons that those who we consider "dead" are not no-longer-existent, but *live* in another part of the One Universe — a plane from which communication is difficult but possible (b) guidance — either specific suggestions to a specific person or persons, or, in the highest sense, teaching relating to the fundamental truths about living.

We know that some great composers and musicians were so greatly talented (that is, their talents were so close to the surface) that they were able to compose meaningful works of music, or perform on musical instruments with great skill and depth of interpretation, at an early age and with a minimum of instruction. But we also know that other such persons who did not, therefore, bother with instruction did not develop far — they stayed on the level at which they started and, for the most part, gradually deteriorated. The great composers and musicians who were what we call "naturals" studied and worked — labored just as hard, perhaps harder, than those whose talents required more training to bring out. Mozart both performed and composed at a very early age; but his earliest compositions show little more than talent. Some of them are charming to listen to; but if we can dispense with the fond illusion that *any* composition signed "Mozart" is therefore a great masterwork, we can hear also that these early works are no better than the general run of good but not outstanding compositions by others in that period who did not have such facility. Had Mozart not bothered to study and labor, he would be known today only by a handful of musicologists specializing in the late 18th century, if any of his work survived at all.

Likewise with psychic talent. The person with "natural" mediumistic ability who goes at once into seances may indeed get results; but the odds are that the communications will not be of a high level — and most likely the sort of thing which most people think of when they think of mediums (assuming that they consider the possibility of a genuine medium at all), meaningless chit-chat with Aunt So-and-so, etc.

Every talent, as is shown in the Parable of the Talents, is a responsibility. What you do with it is far more important than precisely how much you may have.

Most of the communications we receive are Readers' Preference Coupons, with or without comments written in the space provided for them. Letters of comment are put into a separate folder, instead of being kept with the ballots, *unless* the letter writer states clearly that the epistle is not for publication. Sometimes the writer will specify that certain parts are not for publication; in such an instance, these proscribed sections are marked out in red pencil, either to be cut out literally with scissors if the letter is already typed, or not to be transcribed if we are typing a clearly handwritten letter. An ellipsis . . . indicates a deletion.

NO POT SHOTS AT SHERMAN

Dear Mr. Lowndes:

I received the September issue of EXTU today, and was so captivated by the feature articles that I was quite "read out" when I got to *The Eyrie*. The shock of seeing my letter really revived me. I thought I had mentioned in it at the end that the letter was not for publication. Perhaps I failed to include those words *(You did, Miss McKeever; the words were not there, and our telepath wasn't working that day; sorry, RAWL)*, but since the letter was in fact published, I wish to make myself clear about one thing; namely, I was not taking a public pot shot at Harold Sherman. True, I am not impressed with Mr. Sherman's actual accomplishments, but never would I risk offense by stating so in a publication. Now that it has happened, as it did in this issue, I cannot retract my statement.

What I was really annoyed with was having an organization send me a price list of a particular individual's books and records, offering me a discount on same if I became a member of the Clairvoyant Society. The printed material included a membership form, and stated that one could still apply for membership if one did not wish to make a purchase. Apparently no qualifications were necessary except to sign the statement, "I will only use ESP for good," or words close to these. I no longer have that portion of the material, after sending in part of it with a request for information concerning the Clairvoyant Society. The "mail out" material did not include anything pertaining to the Society. My request for more material was never acknowledged. . . . Your comments came close to what I was thinking.

One of the most blood-chilling books I have ever read, namely *The Morning of the Magicians*, by Pauwels and Bergier, concerns the great involvement of the Nazis with occult science, and in this belated glimpse into the hellish minds of the Nazi leaders, there is mention of a statement the German people had to sign when applying for a job. They had to swear that they believed in the "fire and ice" theory which was one of the main tenents of the inner-circle Nazi-Occult Philosophy, the Black Order, whose doctrines all too quickly were reduced to "Believe, obey, fight; that's all."

My original complaint centers upon "*a*" society asking "*an*" individual, qu' · impersonally, to sign . . . a statement so that this individual could become a member of an organization which uses not one word to declare what it is or what its goals are, and which ignores a request for further information. This Society may, in fact, be a worthy one; however, requests for membership in this manner do not invite confidence, for the qualifications are too flimsy if all it takes is a signature to a one-sentence statement. I would certainly demand more than that if I were organizing such a Society. But I am a firm believer in freedom and would not want so much as one

blind, half-blind or so-so follower who might, in the process, lose his germ of creativity by becoming submerged in a group. The value of such a poorly constructed group would only be in yea-saying and nay-saying without bothering to investigate what they are for or against.

May your readers join the 500,000 Europeans who purchased this book, *Morning of the Magicians* (Stein & Day, 7 East 48th Street, NYC) in finding out what was really behind Hitler's rise to power. Some will see how close to the same abyss they are standing.

    — *Evelyn McKeever.* 642 Jones Street, San Francisco, Calif. 94102.

PS — You may publish this letter . . .

And we wish to make clear that we are not taking pot shots at either Mr. Sherman or The Clairvoyant Society, whose aims may indeed be worthy.

Your request for further information may not have been "ignored" in any deliberate, intentional sense; letters do go astray or get lost in this far from perfect world, and sometimes letters received are lost track of. Having been accused myself of "ignoring" letters which I never received, or which actually arrived but got misplaced due to circumstances' being somewhat less than perfect, I hesitate to accuse without more tangible evidence.

It is entirely possible that the signed statement they ask for is only a *preliminary* requirement for membership; and that further tests are required before an applicant is actually admitted, or furnished with anything more than generally available material (material which the person could easily obtain elsewhere without any requirement whatsoever).

The problem of screening applicants is a very tricky one; beyond a certain point (unless persons with sufficient psychic talent to detect really undesirable members are on the applications board, or whatever) one simply has to take some-

one else's word for something. The person who intends to deceive or defraud (and is sure that he can "get away" with it) will not hesitate to sign solemn declarations or take solemn oaths—yet, that is hardly a sufficient reason for eliminating such procedures.

There seems to be a body of opinion these days that requiring a person to state or declare that his motives and intentions are honorable is some sort of tyranny —which strikes your editor as being a rather bizarre idea. If I mean to abide by the rules of a society so long as I am a member of that society (large or small), and desire whatever advantages I believe will come from membership in this society, why should I be reluctant to say so? (However, by the same token, if a society, large or small, desires such a declaration, the society is obligated to inform the applicant clearly exactly what he is pledging loyalty to. It should not be obscure on either side of the agreement.)

DISSENT

Dear Mr. Lowndes:

Having read several recent issues of *EXPLORING THE UNKNOWN,* and found that the articles were written, for the most part, with professional objectivity, it was with shocked disbelief that I read the book review in the April 1966 issue of your magazine written by Jerryl L. Keane, Ph. D., about Harold W. Percival's *Thinking and Destiny.*

As a psycho-therapist by profession, and a student of philosophy, I protest Dr. Keane's assumptions. As a former journalist, I object to her flagrant distortion of the facts of this book.

It is obvious to anyone who has even glimpsed the portent of Mr. Percival's philosophy, that Dr. Keane has not viewed *Thinking and Destiny* with any degree of correct perception or objectivity. How then, can she presume to *review* it? It is evident that Dr. Keane is biased in her presumptions . . .

In the first paragraph of her "review" (?) Dr. Keane states that, "His (Mr. Percival's) works have established another of the 'occult' or 'esoteric' schools. . . ." At no point in *any* of Mr. Percival's writings does he suggest or imply that his conceptions form the basis of any *school, method,* or *system.* To the contrary, Mr. Percival emphasizes the point that each person must find his own individual way to what he terms, "Self-knowledge". According to Mr. Percival's writings, "schools," "methods," and "systems" are obstacles in the course of individual self-advancement.

The third paragraph of Dr. Keane's article begins, "Mr. Percival's emphasis in these teachings is wrapped around not only the idea of attaining adepthood, but of remaining in a physical body permanently." This statement is not merely absurd, it is completely false! Here again, just the opposite of Dr. Keane's statement is true!...

There are other glaring discrepancies throughout the review, but these mentioned suffice to make my point unmistakingly clear.

Subscribing to the axiom that we can take from a page, or from an experience, only what we are capable of bringing to it, the charitable excuse (if excuse, there can be!) for Dr. Keane's uncharitable review of *"Thinking and Destiny,"* is her apparent limited scope of perception . . . and/or experience.

Unfortunately, those among the readers of this "review" who are not acquainted with the profound significance of Mr. Percival's writings may not recognize those limitations. They, then, are the unsuspecting victims of Dr. Keane's reporting....
— *Mrs. Jeanette Miller,* 920 N. California Ave., Palo Alto, Calif.

We deleted our correspondent's comments upon the issue of the condition of Dr. Keane's review copy, as this matter was covered in a previous issue (EXTU, September 1966, page 870).

Writing a book for public consumption is no less a public performance than appearing on the stage or lecture platform, etc., and one takes the risks of boos while one hopes for applause — or at least thoughtful consideration of what has been said. Either assent or dissent may come for the wrong reason.

Criticism is also a public performance, and the critic or reviewer is thus subject to the same risks as the author whose works are being criticised or discussed. It is our policy to give reviewers every possible leeway, and to open our pages to any reader who disagrees; it is also our intention not to permit personal abuse (that is, attack upon the author or the critic rather than the ideas expressed by the author or critic) and where this enters into an otherwise reasonable comment (with which the editor may or may not agree) it is deleted in publication, wherever we are aware of it.

ON THE COMING CHARLES III

Dear Editor:

I was interested in reading a letter in the *Eyrie* from Lumsden, Canada, concerning the future of the British Royal family. Prince Charles' will come to the throne, as he is Scorpio born and Scorpio born generally achieve their inheritance. Perhaps his mother, Elizabeth II, will abdicate in the not too distant away future, as the throne has become a burden to her. However Prince Charles may not remain too long as we see the British Empire disintegrating, the Colonies dropping away and becoming independent.

Elizabeth II, unlike Queen Victoria, takes no part in governering. She lacks the grit of Victoria, who was an autocratic Queen but who asserted prestige of the British Empire, and she hasn't any of the greatness of Elizabeth I, who in that faraway age helped to make Britain the great empire she had become. The present Elizabeth II has none of the prestige of Elizabeth Tudor or of Victoria. Her son may follow in her footsteps and become only a figurehead, but under Scorpio will ascend.

Another letter I enjoyed reading was from P. J. Andrews and I agree with him. We all want Reincarnation as that is the only way we can work our destiny out. The story of Adam and Eve would do many good, if they ciphered it properly. Adam and Eve were put on Earth to live forever, but they sinned and that brought death into the world, so man got to pass down through death and incarnate again from the Spirit; but we also have a Spirit world which I have proof of, as my experiences have proved that to me.
— *Irene Bird,* 1217 Retallack Street, Regina Sask, Canada.

It is possible, even today, for a British sovereign with a strong and winning personality to exert a fair amount of influence; but the throne simply is not what it was in the days of Victoria. The British people, through Parliament, simply would not permit a monarch to be

Many readers inform us that they are unable to find ExPLORING THE UNKNOWN on their local newsstands. We are doing everything we can in order to rectify this deplorable situation, but there are limits to what we can do. If your local dealer cannot obtain EXTU for you, why not take advantage of our subscription offer on page 126 of this issue, which also tells about back issues and their contents? It is not required that you fill out this form in order to subscribe, and save money. Just be sure that your name and address are clearly printed, and that you let us know the date of the latest issue you have, so we can start your subscription with the following number.

"king" or "queen" in the older sense—and without support no one can rule very long.

Yet a British king or queen need not be nothing more than a figurehead. Despite the absence of power even so little as that which Victoria had, George V and George VI were both of great service to the realm; they symbolized the unity and aspirations of a great people, and they both possessed the necessary *charisma* to make this almost a tangible thing to a hard-pressed populace without being actual rulers. Perhaps it is the absence of a challenge which has made the p r e s e n t queen seem somewhat pallid by comparison; those of her family who have been annointed have usually been able to make their presence felt when a crisis came up and the realm looked to the throne for—shall we say psychic inspiration? V i g o r o u s Prime Ministers have been the actual rulers . . . but beyond this, he who wore the crown has still made a difference. Without power, the sovereign has been able in such crisis to rise above party and faction and express the "mystique" of the realm in a way that could be seen and heard. Britain would have been poorer throughout the agony of two wars without this. And I have the feeling that, for all the arguments that can be raised against continuing the monarchy, the British people realize that there is nothing comparable to put in its place. It's rather expensive in cash outlay (though nothing compared to the days when king or queen really ruled) but perhaps they've gotten their money's worth!

In the United States of America, the President combines the power and the mystique of a monarch, without the apparatus; even relatively weak Presidents have still been more than figureheads. . . . I rather suspect that were I British, I might grouse about the monarch as much as anyone else who does so—

Have You Missed These Issues?

Order From Page 129

but not vote against continuing it should the issue actually arise.

REPLY TO DR. MARTELLO

Dear Mr. Lowndes:

In the *Eyrie* (April 1966, page 115), one of your letter writers, a Mr. Leo Louis Martello is taking issue with me. I would have answered sooner if I hadn't been sick. I still stick by my words that human reasoning alone will not bring you into contact with God.

I agree with him that human reasoning is a precious gift from God, and so it is. It was given to us with our other senses to enable us to get along in our earthly surroundings. He must agree that human reasoning can only spring from human experiences, which we learn by trial and sorrow. Would he take the *Kitty Hawk* to break the sound barrier? Then how can he take faulty, finite reasoning to try and reach the infinite and the Divine?

I agree with him about the miserable creatures who allow emotions to tear them apart and feel they must suffer. This is wrong because when you have really found God, you possess the greatest peace and joy. Agreed also that his interpretation is as valid as mine.

I also agree that God represents the best in man. Also it would be a pitiful thing for one not to use his intellect and reason on this material level which we live. That takes care of the material man in his earthly environment, but how about the Spiritual man?

None of us could know life if we didn't have the Spark of God in us; this Spirit in us, which we have all sadly neglected in favor of materialism.

It would be well to remember that the spiritual part of you is also God-given and Jesus Himself preached to the people and warned them time after time that they must be "born again" of the Spirit. And the Spirit in us must be "born again", because obviously man has let it die in him in favor of the flesh. (See 1 Corinthians, 3 — true wisdom, 6 to 16.)

I accuse all those who deny the Divine

(Turn to Page 110)

CLASSIFIED ADVERTISING

EXPLORING THE UNKNOWN will accept such classified advertising for this section as meets with the standards of the publication. Rates are 25c a word for two insertions with name and address to be counted as words. Please send cash with your orders for insertion. Send type set up or typewritten copy.

The classified advertising section of EXPLORING THE UNKNOWN is a fascinating part of our magazine. We know that many of our readers have been helped by these announcements and our advertisers have expressed satisfaction with their results. If you have problems or are interested in specific services and/or articles offered to you, please write to the advertiser and mention that you saw the ad in EXPLORING THE UNKNOWN. It benefits the magazine and helps the advertisers to decide to continue their ads.

BOOKS, MAGAZINES, ETC.

MARGIE ANSWERS YOU! DICTATED FROM SPIRIT WORLD BY MARGIE OF "CHIMES". Most unusual occult book ever written, $3.85 ppd. Order from P. HASTINGS, Box 219OE, Pomona, Calif. 91766.

"DO-IT-YOURSELF ESP TESTING". FASCINATING! ANYONE CAN DO! $2.00 — MAGNETIC, BOX 3677-EUY, WASHINGTON, D. C. 20007.

THE PEYOTE STORY—Actual description of American Indian ceremonies. 43 pages. Illustrated. Collector's item. Special $1.00. Guaranteed. Spencer Books, 3295 Vicotry Center, North Hollywood, Calif. 91609.

FINE BOOKS! Over 2500 Titles. Renowned authors. 15¢ each, ppd. Books on all subjects. Something for everyone. FREE literature. — KEEL, 249 W. 11th Street, New York, N. Y. 10014.

OUT OF THIS WORLD! "MOODOLOGIA", by Solomon Kutakoff. Challenges Psyche and Intellect! Contains his original 28 Interludes. Bonus: FREE, $1.00 copy — 84 Living Passages. Send only $1.20 for both. Write for #7. AuraGraphic Publications, 437 Lyons Avenue, Neward, N.J. 07112.

When answering ads, please mention EXPLORING THE UNKNOWN

BOOKS, MAGAZINES, ETC.

HOW TO SPEAK WITH THE DEAD! AT LAST, YOU WILL LEARN THE TRUTH ABOUT LIFE AND FRIENDS. DISCOVER THE SECRETS OF HEALTH, HAPPINESS, WEALTH AND LOVE. EXPERIENCED MEDIUM REVEALS FOR THE FIRST TIME, SAFE, TESTED, EASY TO FOLLOW STEPS. A PRICELESS VALUE. ONLY $1.00 POSTPAID. WILLIAMSBURG PUBLISHING COMPANY, BOX 118-EB, BROOKLYN, NEW YORK 11203

COUNSELING

TROUBLED? Need advice? Questions answered. $1.00 each. Send birthdate and stamp. Sylvia Smallwood. 5105 Benning, El Paso, Texas 79904

MONEY, LOVE, SUCCESS through Divine Power! Confidential. Charles Redmond, Box 8454 HK, Los Angeles, Calif. 90008.

PERSONAL

CRYSTAL CLEAR, concise, nothing superfluous. Distilled from the greatest esoteric teachings both ancient and modern. Develop your ESP gives the exact technique $2.00. The Magic Matrix, passed on from one of America's greatest spiritually and scientifically gifted geniuses, explains how to create new situations through matrixal thinking. Gleaned from a book that sells for over $100, price $3.00. Save yourself ten years of wasted searching and experimenting. If you don't know these things you will remain the pawn of those that do. Evelyn McKeever, 642 Jones Street, San Francisco, Calif. 94102. In response to many inquiries, yes, I will direct my developed intuitive faculties to your problems or questions. Enclose $1.00 service charge. No personal visits, please.

Read about me in "The Power of Prophecy" by Brad Steiger.

PERSONAL

"DO-IT-YOURSELF ESP TEST ING". Fascinating! Simplified, step-by-step method. HOW TO TEST YOURSELF FOR EXTRASENSORY PERCEPTION! Explains Mental Telepathy, Clairvoyance, Precognition, Psychokinesis. $2.00. MAGNETIC, Box 3677-EUZ, Washington, D. C. 200007.

SEEK CELESTIAL FAVOUR as Ancients did! Original Formula with Mystic Incense, $2. PURIFY YOURSELF with food and drink used in Biblical times: Scientifically proven to aid health and Longevity. Complete information, $2. HIGH BLOOD PRESSURE? Get fast, sure relief! PROLONG LIFE! Herbalist's advice $2.00. Guaranteed. — "MARCO". 24 John North, (Dept: E), Hamilton, Ontario, Canada

LECTURES

DR. JERRYL L. KEANE holds a weekly lecture series in Fairfield, Conn., with round table discussion following the talk. She is also available for talks to club or church groups in the Southern Connecticut and New York City areas. For details write to Box 655, South Norwalk, Conn. 06856.

SPIRITUAL HEALING

IN NEED OF HELP? There is a power that is ever available regardless of who or where you are. WELCOME THIS DIVINE SOURCE. There is nothing you cannot accomplish; be it Spiritual, Financial, or Physical. Send for information and enclose self-addressed and stamped envelope. THE HEALING PRESENCE, Box 407, Latham, N. Y.

Absent Spiritual Healing Treatments. Certified I. M. S. Practitioner. Rev. W. R. Harrison, Ms. T. D. Box 551E, Harding Highway, Newfield, N. J. 08344. Love Offering. 5c stamp.

SPIRITUAL HEALING — Devoted to my work. N. Biglow, Box 113, N. E. Station, Livonia, Michigan, 48152.

MIND-OVER MATTER

NEW PSYCHIC DISCOVERY MicroBionic Torque Meter demonstrates that your mind will easily move distant objects without physical contact! World's only device for developing mind-over-matter! Instrument kit assembled in two hours. $5.00 postpaid. MICROBIONIC LABORATORY, #2 Heritage Hill, Tuscaloosa, Alabama.

When answering ads, please mention EXPLORING THE UNKNOWN

When answering ads, please mention EXPLORING THE UNKNOWN

Have You Missed These Issues?

June 1962: *Joan of Arc and the Supersensible* by Jeanne de Mare; *Can Witches Kill?* by Dean Lipton; *Reincarnated Spirits Within Me* by Retha M. Sales.

Aug. 1962: *What is Radiesthesia?* by Mary Elsnau; *The Sampford Apparition* by H. R. Dreyer; *Spiritual Speaking* by Robert A. W. Lowndes.

Oct. 1962: *The Somerville Communication* by Geraldine Cummins; *Infinity Equals Evolution* by Jerryl L. Keane; *Limitations* by Robert A. W. Lowndes.

Dec. 1962: *More Worlds Than One* by Jerryl L. Keane; *Bougon's Permanent Magnetic Motion* by Gaston Burridge; *Something in the Snow* by Edward Hoch.

Feb. 1963: *ESP and Obscure Psychoses* by R. C. Connell, M.D., F. R. C. P.; *Houdini and the Spirits* by Lydia Emery *Astrology As A Science* by Robert A. W. Lowndes.

Apr. 1963: *Diagnosis by ESP* by R. C. Connell, M.D., F. R. C. P; *Something In The Smoke,* by Edward D. Hoch; *The Uses of Astrology,* by Robert A. W. Lowndes.

June 1963: *The Great Satanist Plot,* by L. Sprague de Camp; *The Lost King Of France* by Barber & Hoeller; *Who Wants Reincarnation?* by Robert A. W. Lowndes.

Aug. 1963: *The Healers Of England,* by Jerryl L. Keane; *The Land Of Ghosts and Witches,* by the Rev. Stephan A. Hoeller, D. D.; *Haunted By The Living,* by Dr. Nandor Fodor.

Order From Page 129

(Continued from Page 98)

Spirit within them, those who deny its existence, and its power to lift up above mere mortal senses. It would be well to remember that the development of one's spirit is the "building one's house on rock", while exclusive development of the flesh and its senses is the "building on sand".

As for telling "those with superior 'inner vision'" to go to an eye bank" . . . "inner vision" is of the Spirit; it has nothing to do with mortal eyes, and if God so chose, He could let you see even through an eye doctor would say that the eyes were lifeless and dead.

Yes — do use your eyes to see and your ears to hear and your mind to think — about the all-important Spiritual side of your nature.

— *Vida C. Schneider,* 77 Chester Place, Yonkers 4, N.Y. 10704.

Jesus declared, "the kingdom of heaven is within you", and He also said to those who followed Him, "the things I do, you shall do also". He further stated that not everyone who just called Him "Lord" and in other ways went through empty motions of being a follower or disciple was really "of" His followers. It seems to this writer that these add up to an affirmation of the same Divine teachings that have issued from innumerable other prophets and teachers; and one (just one among many) implication is that the Power of God (which includes that Healing Power called "miraculous") is also within each and every one of us; we need but to contact It. It is not something separate and remote; we do not need some other channel — although some other person or persons may play a very vital role in helping us to find this Power within us. Further, our ability to contact and open our "separated" selves to this God power is something which has to be developed; and this involves the spiritual rebirth Jesus spoke of. Since none of us is entirely sufficient unto himself, we are all called to help each other see, hear, respond, develop; but while *any* other human being may minister unto me in this fashion, no one (nor all of humanity in concert) can respond and develop *for* me.

There's a fable about the man who dreamed that he had gone to "hell"; he found himself in a large room, wherein was a table filled to overflowing with all manner of delicious food. Around the table was an assembly of gaunt and obviously starving men and women. Each had a long fork—too long to get into his mouth, and each was struggling helplessly, often stabbing his neighbors in the process.

Then the man dreamed that he was translated to "heaven"; and he found himself in the same sort of room, with the same sort of table, and the men and women around it all looking well fed and happy— yet they had the same sort of impossible forks that the dwellers in "hell" had.

What made the difference? In "heaven" they were feeding each other!

P.S.— But each one had to do his own chewing and swallowing.

OBJECTION ...

Dear RAWL:

From the tone of several of her last articles, I assume that Doctor Keane is a woman. This explains a lot of things. For instance, my inability to follow some of her logic. I know that you know as well as I, that regardless of the subject, women just do not think like men. No offense meant, of course.

However, this basic assumption is strengthened by examination of her latest literary journey into the mist of the little known — not because of the subject — but because of the treatment. This article which appeared in the July issue of EXTU, entitled: *Parapsychology — the Great Evasion* labors on for 14 pages.

At first glance fully one half of the article

Have You Missed These Issues?

Oct. 1963: *The Poltergeist Of Slawensik*, by Pauline Saltsman; *The Way Of Dreams*, by Jack Willis; *Thirteen Witnesses*, by Jerryl L. Keane.

Jan. 1964: *People Who Disappear*, by Brad Steiger; *The Law of Eternal Progress* by Jerryl L. Keane, Phd.D.; *The Greater Reality* by Robert A. W. Lowndes.

Apr. 1966: *What 'Voodoo' Really Is*, by Madam Arboo; *The Inner Realm*, by Joel S. Goldsmith; *Why I Became A Healer*, by The Rev. Florian Magiera.

June 1964: *Thoughts In Orbit*, by Vincent H. Gaddis; *The Last Druid?* by Paul Johnstone; *The True Art Of Magick* by Margaret Bruce.

Oct. 1964: *Louisa: The Story of A Hex*, by E. Linder Nalesnyk, *An Introduction To Astrology*, by Beatrice Epstein; *Something in Salem*, by Edward D. Hoch.

Dec. 1964: *The Man Who Could See The Future*, by Dean Lipton; *Grandfather's Ghost*, by E. Linder Nalesnyk; *Tapping The Mind's Power*, by James C. Rogers.

Feb. 1965: *Are Human Vampires Real?* by Joachim Heinrich Woos; *Body Rhythms and Present Knowledge*, by Jerryl L. Keane, Ph.D.; *Houses That Harbor Hatred*, by Brad Steiger.

May 1965: *The Howl of Death*, by E. Linder Nalesnyk; *Of Duration and Sequence*, by Jerryl L. Keane, Ph.D.; *Frank Robinson*, by Robert A. W. Lowndes.

Order From Page 129

Have You Missed These Issues?

Order From Page 129

is devoted to epitomizing those from the past (whose imagination could conceivably fill in where memory leaves off); people long dead whose writings have lost nothing in transformation into modern print; people whose experiences or beliefs reinforce the good Doctor's own beliefs. Which, I suppose, is the only way an article of this type could be handled. It is only natural then, to sprinkle throughout the piece bits and pinches of past or recent facts to liven up the brew.

However, the other half, I fear, is greatly to her discredit. It flys from complaintive protest to scathing attacks on the mental soundness of persons as equally erudite as she; persons who do not accept for a scientific fact the existence of sixth sense phenomena without believable evidence. Most learned men are extremely cautious about taking a stand over a once-in-a-lifetime experience, or unrepeatable experiments. Although, at this point, someone may argue that if these investigators believe nothing they read, how can they know anything? The counter-argument is that those with higher education, as a rule, can reconstruct experiments and results from what they studied in books — with the possible exception of psychology. In fact, IBM engineers have built the actual devices conceived by Leonardo da Vinci.

Fortunately, the targets of these diatribial hexes (we don't know who, since no names were mentioned), do at least suspect that ESP phenomena is worth investigation. Their suspicion is enough at least to attempt to devise reliable tests (feeble fumblings perhaps) designed to provide believable evidence of the little understood phenomena of the mind.

Even so, these skeptics, should not be condemned outright for refusing to accept unreservedly something which to them is little more than sayso of persons ten times removed from the present day. As a case in point: I have tens of thousands of articles on UFO phenomena witnessed by reliable persons. The Air Force employs professional skeptics to pooh-pooh away a great number of these news articles. They use explanations which I consider ridiculous; however, I do not condemn them, since every man, or woman, has a per-

Want a Free Book?

That's what members of the Psychic Book Society, who joined at its inception, are really getting. By becoming a member — there are no entrance fees — you receive important psychic books *before* publication date. And you get a 25 percent discount, so you also save money. On four books you save more than enough to buy that extra one. You get five books for the price of four.

Members who received the first four books issued have saved $2.00 compared with what ordinary customers must pay. So they have enough to buy an extra book. The current release is "Nothing So Strange", an autobiography of world-famous medium Arthur Ford. Members pay only $2.00 for this book including postage.

If that isn't sufficient to convince you of the Society's value, take a look at the titles so far issued: "When a Child Dies", by Sylvia Barbanell; "Out of This World", by J. Bernard Hutton; "The Psychic Life of Jesus", by the Rev. Maurice Elliott; "Guidance From Silver Birch", edited by Anne Dooley.

Members not only benefit from this Society's special offer, they also help get important books into print. Each book is in hard covers, identical to those sold later at their full price. The Society plans to publish four books a year, generally not exceeding $2.50. For each a member pays only $2.00 including postage. Start saving NOW. Complete and sign the form below.

-------------------- CUT HERE --------------------

To The Psychic Book Society, 23 Great Queen Street, London, W.C.2.

Please enrol me as a member of the Psychic Book Society. I agree to purchase the books published by the Society at the special discount of 25 per cent plus the cost of postage.

NAME ....
(PLEASE USE BLOCK CAPITALS)   (State if Mrs., Miss or Mr.)

ADDRESS ....

....

....

SIGNATURE...

fect right to his own opinion — whether or not he is a so-called expert.

Our skeptical parapsychology researchers should instead be tolerated by those who know for sure in their first gropings toward the light. The parapsychological field could sure use some additional supporters, even if their methods are left handed. Most of the people I know, when I mention ESP, telekinesis, clairvoyance, etc., act as if I might be ready for the men in the white coats. Consequently, it pays to use discretion when mentioning these subjects.

And as for newspapers and other news media devoting more space for spiritual healing and similar things, that's a laugh. Newsmen are not known for even believing that which they see with their own eyes, much less believing in something as nebulous as extra sensory phenomena, per se. Although, this is not to say there are none sympathetic as witnessed by the enclosed article.

If my search of truth was not always driving my thoughts, and I had not read about or heard of ESP phenomena before, Doctor Keane's scattergun attack on skeptics would cause me to entertain serious doubts as to parapsychology's credibility.

But all is not as black as the good Doctor would have us believe — and here I enclose a brochure of a new book. I ask you to judge for yourself.
— *Ira D. Adams, Jr.,* 3001 Kirkland Dr., Huntsville, Alabama

...AND REPLY

Dear Rawl:

Thanks for passing Mr. Ira D. Adams, Jr.'s letter along to me.

I'm terribly sorry that he did not like what I wrote, but his opening paragraph struck me as rather funny. My sex has never been any secret to regular EXTU readers, I know, for you have done several short biographies of me in the past. However, I don't know that I particularly consider my sex anybody's business but my own; and after something over twenty years as a designer draftsman in engineering, I realize that people who base either intelligence and/or reasoning power on sex are giving not only an adequate demonstration of their own intelligence and reasoning power, but the direction of their thinking.

The gentleman is either assuming that I know as little as he apparently does about this subject, or that his knowledge extends to its full scope. I don't feel that he really read the article; and while I have gone over the prospectus for the book which he sent, and (basing my impressions on this prospectus, as I have not seen the book), it seems to me that this is precisely the sort of thing that I am talking about: The scientists today who claim they are investigating this simply do not know, or do not want to know, what they are looking for.

I would suggest to the gentleman that he spend his next vacation in England, start his own investigations at the SAGB in Belgrave Square, go from there down to the NFSH in Shere (at Edward's Sanctuary), pick up a few of the big meetings, such as a couple of the healing meetings, perhaps Phil Wyndham's, and a couple of the big demonstration meetings, perhaps Stan Poulton's or Joe Benjamin's, and then circulate around a few of the churches and see what there is to see. A couple of weeks of this would bring him into what I *am* talking about, rather than what he thinks I am talking about.

I would also suggest that instead of announcing himself as an American investigator, he just go and snoop and confine his conversation to confirmation of the evidence given him if he understands it and questions about it if he doesn't. I'm not doing a "scattergun attack on the skeptics", because I feel that one should investigate carefully, eliminating all material which is in any way dubious; but until he has seen what I have seen, and experienced similar occurences, he will not understand that there is a difference between "belief" and "knowledge"; and I do not believe, *I know — from first hand experience,* which is obviously something which he has not had.

Also, as far as "erudition" goes, he may not realize it, but there tends to be an inverse proportion here, for what we call "education" often results in stultification of the wider senses. I wish him success in his search for truth.
— *Jerryl L. Keane,* Ph.D.

The Swap Corner

This department is a free service for you, the readers, and we shall run it whenever we have material from you on hand at the time that we have to get copy for the issue off to our printer. The rule is that nothing here is to be listed for sale, but for exchange only; and EXPLORING THE UNKNOWN assumes no responsibility for arrangements that you, the readers, make with each other. Be sure that your name and address is printed clearly in your listings, if you are unable to type the copy you want us to run.

Dear Swappers:

I have to swap occult and flying saucer books, for some I've not read — new and in good condition.

— *Dr. Elizabeth Reams,* 2113 East 45th Street, North Plaee, Nebraska, 69101.

Dear Sir:

Please include the following in your Swap Corner.

Have hundreds of scarce books on lost continents, archaeology, and the occult to trade for books on lost continents, the inner earth theory, flying saucers, and the strange in general.

— *F. D. Brownley,* 29 McCall Road, Rochester, New York 14615.

Dear Sirs:

I would appreciate it if you can include this in a future Swap Column.

Wanted - Photos, clippings, pamphlets, bulletins, magazines, and books on UFO's especially the following: EC Flying Saucer Report, Space Probe, Space Review, Flying Saucers & The Three Men, Bender Mystery Confirmed, Flying Saucerama,

Index To Volume Six

The Dates of these issues are September 1965, December 1965, February 1966, April 1966, July 1966, and September 1966. (F) indicates "filler", an item which appears at the end of some article to fill out space, and thus occupies less than a full page. (BR) indicates "book review"; the title of the book is given in italics, while the author, editor, translator, etc., is indicated in parentheses.

The Ignorant Explorer

(Continued from page 9)

why waste your time following bees around, except to search out their honeycombs?

"Great scientists make great discoveries. But individually, they make few per lifetime, and they do not make them on demand. 'Necessity is the mother of invention' applies mostly to ingenious applications, not to fundamental discoveries. Doc (Edward Elmer) Smith had the right formula right in *The Skylark of Space*. Richard Seaton discovered a metal, X, with remarkable properties. Then all the gadgets arose logically out of this one discovery. Furthermore, most of the original sets of gadgets were actually reduced to practice in collaboration with Crane, the engineer, not solely by Seaton, the pure scientist. This is the way it is is life . . ."—from *Scientists in Science Fiction*, by Philip R. Geffe.

HERE IS the aspect of science: the application of discovery. We separate the two functions by calling the discoverer the "pure" scientist, while we call the person who figures out ways to make use of it, constructing gadgets which work on the principles the pure scientist has uncovered, an "engineer". In the larger sense, both are scientists, both seek the laws of the universe, but in different ways—the one to find out what they are, the other to find out what they can be for.

Our first quotation also deals with engineering. In the story, Vergil was following a process, a precise, detailed set of instructions, worked out by engineering. The process, as the story relates, included not only physical ingredients and mixing and handling formulas, but also the wearing of certain types of clothing, the recitation of certain ritual prayers, etc.

And here is superstition—obvious, is it not? Yet . . . is it really obvious?

Where does the superstition lie?

Again in the failure to ask "why"; again in becoming content with a partial answer.

But be not too eager to be content with the "obvious" fault. Because history shows that one reason why the old-time philosopher-magician-scientists insisted that certain prayers, etc., were necessary, was because experience showed that things went wrong — sometimes disasterously wrong — when they were altered or omitted.

Did anyone try to see if a process would work without the prayers, but with everything else as instructed, *provided that everyone trying was convinced that it was possible?*

Probably not — for the very good reason that you couldn't find someone who was really free of crippling doubts in that area. When there is a deep fear of failure, that fear will result in errors that otherwise might be avoidable.

If you really believe that a prayer is necessary (subconsciously) then when you omit it you will be tense; you will not be operating at top efficiency. If delicate operations are required, then the odds are that this very tension will botch them.

And what is more natural than to assume, "See — the prayers are absolutely essential!" And you're entirely right — so long as you believe they are essential, *they are essential!*

So engineering trembles on the brink of superstition when process becomes ceremony. Part of the alchemist's process was engineering; a lot of it was ceremony.

There's nothing wrong with ceremony so long as it isn't confused with ultimate truth.

The old tendency to decide that at last we have all the answers, or at least all the answers we need, leads to "Why look farther? This works, doesn't it?"

Sorry—No Room This Time!

Whenever one of our departments is omitted from an issue of EXPLORING THE UNKNOWN, we receive inquires from readers as to whether the department has been discontinued. Due to the difficulties attending a change-over in printers, we were not able to get **Psychic Experiences** into the November issue; and, alas, it was crowded out this time. Your optimistic editor still hasn't learned that type isn't rubber! We had to leave several other items out this time, among them Dr. Martello's fascinating exploration of the meaning behind the manner in which we cross our "t"s when writing. Next issue (somehow we seem to recall making this vow before) we won't send off so much to be set up in the first place! RAWL

The Natural Philosophers (as scientists were called up to the nineteenth century) had one thing in common: they were not content with the answers already on hand. That something worked just wasn't enough; they wanted to find out *why* it worked — and they wanted to see if something else might not work better, or if some part of the "given" process would turn out to be ceremony after all.

Is there a prescription against superstition in either of the two senses we've been talking about?

Yes — quite a few, in the sense that the prescription has been stated by many different people, in different words:

Over a mosque somewhere in Asia or Africa, I do not recall which, there is an inscription which translates to: "Jesus, on Whom be Peace, has said, 'This life is a bridge; ye are to pass over it, not to build houses upon it.'"

Heracleitus said, "Everything flows . . .

Giordano Bruno preached relativity; Einstein worked out mathematical formulas relating to it.

None of them considered that there was any necessary antagonism between genuine science and genuine religion. When either science or religion becomes a set of dogmas, the final answer to everything, that which is not to be questioned, etc., then science is no less likely to become superstition than a particular religious group, members of which sincerely believe that they represent the one and only true faith.

The God that genuine religion proclaims is a God of law and order, etc., Who can be trusted not to suspend or violate the laws of His creation in order to prove them true. No particular faith or group proclaims Him fully; yet each viewpoint has something valuable to offer. This one, that one, may not have much for me — but it will have much for someone else.

Why?

God is Absolute, Infinite, All, Eternal, Ultimate, etc. .

We are finite, partial, immediate, etc.

The ocean is in the bucket, in the drop taken from it; but the bucketfull, the drop, is not the ocean.

God is in us as the ocean is in the bucketful, the drop; and in that sense, as Jesus, Buddha, etc., said, we are gods.

We see the Infinite, etc., manifested in the finite around us, yet there are those who, seeing, do not see; hearing, do not hear, etc.

And when the eyes are closed, the ears stopped, science no less than religion becomes superstition and engineering bogs down in ceremony.

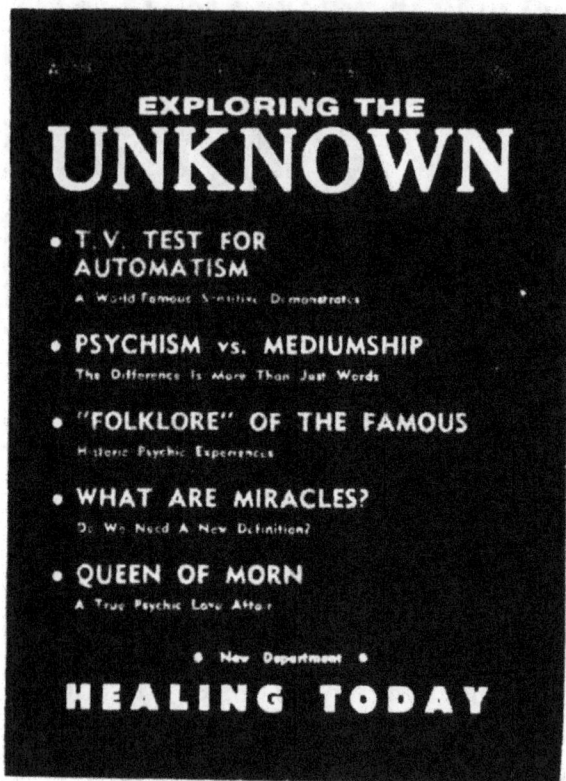

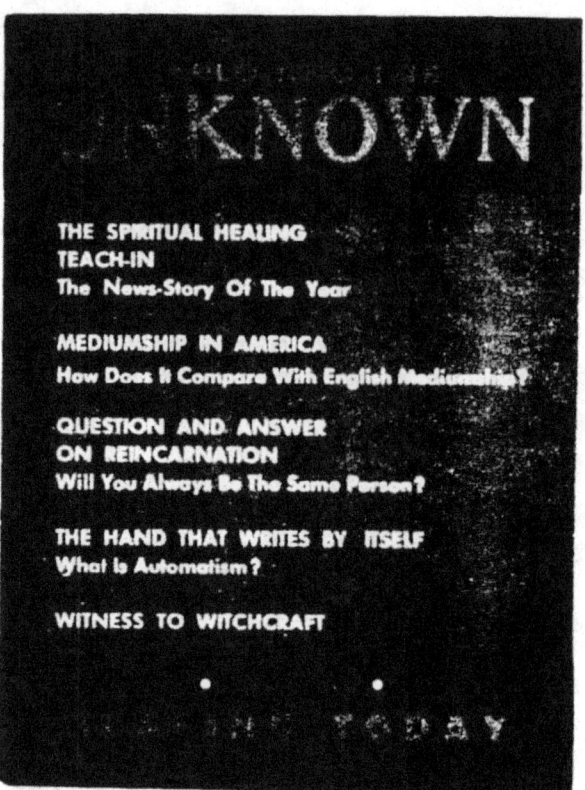

A subscription to EXPLORING THE UNKNOWN will assure you of getting your copy as each issue comes off the press. No need to wait for newsdealer to reorder if he sells out before you get your copy. Price $2.50 per year (6 issues) in U. S., Canada and the Pan American Union. Foreign $3.00. Fill out the coupon below and rush it in NOW.

- -

HEALTH KNOWLEDGE
119 Fifth Avenue
New York, N. Y. 10003

If you do not want to cut this page, use fascimile of coupon.

Please put me down for a year's subscription to *EXPLORING THE UNKNOWN* starting with the issue following the January, 1967 issue. I am enclosing .... (amount). *Please Print.*

Name ....

Address ....

City/State/Zip No. ....

Reader's Preference Page

(there's more space on the flip side)

Comment — Suggested subjects, etc.

_____

_____

_____

_____

_____

_____

_____

_____

_____

_____

_____

YOU CAN HELP US THIS WAY: If you considered a particular item or items outstanding — better than just "first place" — mark a O beside such item or items; then those you considered next best should be marked 1, 2, 3, etc. If you disliked an item or items put an X beside the item or items, so we'll be able to tell dislike from least enjoyed. You may tie as many items as you like; all ties will count as you rate them. We love it if all the items are rated, but so long as two different symbols appear on the voting coupon — or in your letter or postcard — we can score your ballot.

Mail this coupon to EXPLORING THE UNKNOWN, c/o Health Knowledge, Inc., 119 Fifth Avenue, New York, N. Y. 10003
(or better still, write us a letter!)

Reader's Preference Page
(there's more space on the flip side)

See suggestions on other side of the coupon

DID THE PHARAOHS BUILD STONEHENGE?

HINTS ON MEDIUMISTIC DEVELOPMENT

FLYING SAUCERS AND THE CONTACT ENIGMA

THE GREAT EXILE

HEALING SPIRITS

ODD FACTS OF SCIENCE

THE IGNORANT EXPLORER

THE COGITATOR'S CORNER

HEALING TODAY

LOVE vs. love

BOOKS

THE EYRIE

Did you find the cover attractive?   Yes .... No ....

Have You Missed Any of Our Previous Issues?

Many readers have asked us if back issues of EXPLORING THE UNKNOWN are still available. The answer is — yes, for the time being, they are; but some issues are not so plentiful as they were. While they last, they can all be had for the cover price of 50c per copy, postpaid.

Health Knowledge, Inc., Dept. 38,
119 Fifth Avenue, New York, N. Y. 10003

Please send me the following issues of EXPLORING THE UN
KNOWN. I am enclosing   (50¢ per copy.)

Jan. 1960	Aug. 1961	Dec. 1962	June 1964	Feb. 1966
Mar. 1960	Oct. 1961	Feb. 1963	Oct. 1964	Apr. 1966
June 1960	Dec. 1961	Apr. 1963	Dec. 1964	July 1966
Aug. 1960	Feb. 1962	June 1963	Feb. 1965	Sept. 1966
Oct. 1960	Apr. 1962	Aug. 1963	May 1965	Nov. 1966
Jan. 1961	June 1962	Oct. 1963	July 1965	
Apr. 1961	Aug. 1962	Jan. 1964	Sept. 1965	
June 1961	Oct. 1962	Apr. 1964	Dec. 1965	

Name ....

Address ....

City/State/Zip No. ....

www.ingramcontent.com/pod-product-compliance
Lightning Source LLC
Chambersburg PA
CBHW080958020726
47505CB00009B/2255